The Monological Jew

L. S. Dembo

The Monological Jew

A Literary Study

The University of Wisconsin Press

The University of Wisconsin Press
114 North Murray Street
Madison, Wisconsin 53715

The University of Wisconsin Press, Ltd.
1 Gower Street
London WC1E 6HA, England

Copyright ©1988
The Board of Regents of the University of Wisconsin System
All rights reserved

First printing

Printed in the United States of America

5 4 3 2 1

Library of Congress Cataloging-in-Publication Data

Dembo, L. S.
 The monological Jew.
 Bibliography: pp. 186–190.
 Includes index.
 1. American literature—Jewish authors—History and criticism. 2. Jews in literature. I. Title.
PS153.J4D46 1988   810'.9'35203924   87-40517
ISBN 0-299-11680-8
ISBN 0-299-11684-0 (pbk.)

To my father, my sister,
and the memory of my mother

Contents

Preface ix

Acknowledgments xi

Introduction 3

PART ONE. DISTANCE AND RELATION
1. Sartre and the Existential Jew   15
2. Buber and the Dialogical Jew   26

PART TWO. THE MONOLOGICAL JEW IN FICTION
3. Stern's Silent Monologue   35
4. The Tenants of Moonbloooo-ooo   44
5. Carnivalizing the Logos   54
6. The New Jersey Jews and Their Pagan Gods   68
7. David Schearl in the Polyphonic World   76
8. Levinsky and the Language of Acquisition   84
9. The Family Moskat's Descent into Randomness   93

PART THREE. FALSE GODS, GRAVEN IMAGES
10. Art and Idolatry   103
11. Asher Lev: The Mariolatry of a Hasid   112

Contents

12 Reznikoff's Dispersion 117
13 The Objectivist Jew 130

PART FOUR. ANTI-SEMITISM AND THE
MONOLOGICAL GENTILE

14 Pedagogy and/or Pedagoguery: Pound's Way 141
15 Hemingstein: The Way It Wasn't 152
16 The Polyphonic Persecution of Yakov Bok 162

Notes 175
Works Cited 186
Index 191

Preface

I originally intended to write only a series of essays on Jewish themes; I did not aspire to see them bound by a consistent theory into a unified book. I felt that insofar as Jewish-American literature has scarcely gone unnoticed by many capable critics, both Jewish and gentile, my own contribution could be best represented in an informal, if not casual, discussion. Furthermore, I saw no reason to undertake a literary history when there were available such works as Sol Liptzin's *The Jew in American Literature,* Louis Harap's *The Image of the Jew in American Fiction,* now updated to the mid-eighties by *In the Mainstream,* and Leslie Fiedler's *The Jew in the American Novel.* Moreover, I did not wish to challenge the ideas of critics like Irving Howe, Max Schulz, Irving Malin, Jules Chametzsky, Ben Siegel, and Ruth Wisse, who have provided the sociological and cultural overviews by which Jewish writing in America has been understood.

In any case, a central motif and a particular point of view soon began to emerge and to dominate my thinking. Derived from the thought of Martin Buber, and to a lesser extent that of M. M. Bakhtin, the Monological Jew is an abstraction, a philosophic and literary category, that I have pursued for whatever insights it offers about Jewish literature and Jews in general. I am not, I know, the first to approach this subject through Buber; Robert Kegan's *Buber, Bellow, and Malamud* and Peter Hayes' essay on Buber and *The Assistant* are only two instances of the interest in this philosopher.

Thus, far from applying Buber's philosophy systematically to the fiction or tracing his influence on the writer, I have taken what in modern parlance can be called a synchronic approach; I attempt to define a paradigm, whose variations appear throughout a number of texts and these texts take their significance from their relation to each other, not in relation to other books in the author's canon except those in which the paradigm may reappear. Accordingly, I have dealt with only enough novels to illustrate my point. Even though I would like to have offered readings of, say, Stanley Elkin, Cynthia Ozick, Tillie Olsen and Grace Paley as well as a fuller discussion of Saul Bellow, who appears now only in a long footnote, I chose rather to develop a conception that I believed brought an additional dimension of meaning to "monologism"—that of "aesthetic idolatry." It was an idea that interested Ozick and one that I myself had touched upon in an essay on the poetry of Charles Reznikoff (here reprinted as Chapter Twelve). Finally, I examine the gentile counterpart to the Monological Jew, a depressing prospect that both morally and philosophically had to be faced.

Acknowledgments

I am indebted to my wife, Royce, who alone knew what it would take and wouldn't let me stop even after it was all taken; to my colleagues Phillip Harth, Walter Rideout, Howard Weinbrot, Eric Rothstein, Susan Stanford Friedman, and Joseph Wiesenfarth for their friendship and support; to Barbara Hanrahan, Jack Kirshbaum, and Sam Diman of the University of Wisconsin Press whose professionalism and sympathy made working with them a pleasure; to my assistants Sarah Gomez and Steve Luebke, both far overqualified for the job. I am especially grateful to Elaine Kauvar and Alan Wilde for seeing in this book all I had hoped I had put there and much I hadn't dared hope for.

Chapter 12 first appeared as "Objectivist or Jew? Charles Reznikoff in the Diaspora," in *Charles Reznikoff: Man and Poet*, edited by Milton Hindus (Orono: National Poetry Foundation, 1984). Part of the Oppen section of chapter 13 originally appeared as the introduction to "Oppen on His Poems: A Discussion," in *George Oppen: Man and Poet*, edited by Burton Hatlen (Orono: National Poetry Foundation, 1981). Both items are reprinted by permission.

The Monological Jew

Introduction

A monologist, as we all know, is somebody who talks too much and never listens. Babbler, orator, or narrator out of touch with his audience, he is anyone for whom speech is not a means of mutual understanding or communication but the opportunity to perform, to use language for its own sake or to create an impression—in short, for any purpose that does not involve dialogue. People who speak from an obsession are monologists; so are those speaking at cross-purposes. Authority, when beyond appeal, speaks in monologue—as do its propagandists. But so, in a way, do those who have lost faith in authority, especially divine authority, insofar as no longer hoping to turn to God again, they turn only to themselves. Both the transcendental realist and the solipsist, the dogmatist and the cynic, speak from inaccessible positions in which no questioning or other interchange takes place.

As portrayed in fiction these persons, men and women, are often "wordsmen." Voluble, exuberant, and always articulate, they regard language as the device with which life's encounters are met and survived. The difference between the wordsman who is an artist and one who is a candy vendor on trains (Wallant's *Tenants of Moonbloom*) is a matter of degree, not of kind. They both are formalists, who, preoccupied with the medium, not the text, replace a lost ethical reality with an "aesthetic" one, a theological order with a linguistic one. Their God is not YHWH, who remains hidden and resists all attempts to name him, but the very letters of the name itself—that is to say, "language" or utterance. For the artist the golden calf, that archetype of idolatry, is words and decoration; for the candy hawker it is words and money—Apollo or Mammon. Whichever one, the calf is, as the Old Testament would have it, a graven image, a false god, created out of fear and loss of faith by the children of Israel when Moses failed to return in due time from his "dialogue" with the true God. In its current incarnation it is still a creation of fear and trembling, but now in the face of a silent God and a Logos that conveys no message—it may also be, however, a creation of exuberance and that, from a traditional point of view, makes it so much the worse.

What, then, is a "Monological *Jew*?" A useful abstraction even though it covers a multiplicity of characteristics, not all of which are coordinate with each other. To begin with, it refers to a Jew of the Diaspora who has abandoned monotheism but who, having thus removed the mind and soul of Judaism, still feels himself to be a Jew—and yet not a Jew. This figure in search of himself is, of course, a historical and sociological phenomenon; I am interested in him as a philosophical and literary phenomenon, mostly as the latter even though I regard the former essential. Thus as a framework or context for this chiefly literary study I have used a nontechnical reading of Martin Buber's conceptions of dialogue and monologue and of the I-Thou, I-It relations. I have also drawn peripherally on the ideas of monologue, polyphony, and carnivalization of M. M. Bakhtin, the Russian literary critic currently in vogue.

As a point of departure, however, I found the existentialism of Jean-Paul Sartre to be of particular value in that it presents a view of experience that is antithetical to Buber's and therefore throws it into sharp relief. In his theory of the hostile Other, in his orientation to an individualist ethos, and above all in his explicit atheism, Sartre stands in diametrical opposition to Buber, who sees the Other as an intimate, takes communality as the ideal for human behavior, and finally—needless to say—is no atheist. Buber's theory of the I-Thou, the ideal mode of address from one person to another and an indication of the ideal relation "between man and man," has a counterpart in the theory of the I-It, in which the other is reduced to a thing. The I-It marks the *distance* between men and is associated with everyday life in a competitive society; this is the totality—the atomized totality—of the existential world as Sartre depicted it in his pre-Marxist days. The I-Thou marks the *relation* or meeting of man and man, each in his whole person and in intense awareness of the *presence* of the other.

Whether Jew or gentile, the monologist lives in the I-It relation and is therefore a parallel to the Existential Man as Sartre conceives him. Or would be if all other things were equal. But they are not: the Existential Man is a "negativity"; his consciousness separates him from Being and his uncommitted "freedom" completes his nihilation. He is a nothing who is given identity only by the judgment of his fellows. This view dictates Sartre's image of the Jew, whom he sees as being basically the creature of anti-Semitism; and Sartre is eventually led to classifying Jews as authentic and inauthentic, categories that describe the Jew bent on complete assimilation (an impossibility) or the Jew who accepts his situation and his historical role as sufferer.

I am compelled to add that if this argument is determined by existential logic, it seems to be no less a product of Sartre's ignorance of Judaism and Jewish history. Failing to take account of the living, positive elements, of understanding the Jews as actual people and not abstractions, Sartre's whole rationale is simplistic (see *Anti-Semite and Jew*). Even so, it does have something to tell us about the "situation" of the Jew who, renouncing monotheism, finds himself in a state approaching "nausea" as he beholds the randomness or gratuity into which things and language have fallen. Again, this relation to the world is the equivalent of Buber's I-It; in this world there are no I-Thou relations or authentic dialogical moments; hearing only his own voice, each finds not the meaning for all carried by Logos but only the private meaning he determines for himself.[1]

Committed only to words and performance or manipulation, not to communication, the Monological Jew is an exile in all facets of his life—a self-absorbed loner compelled to endure *distance from,* never *relation to,* others. That is to say, he inhabits not only a literal diaspora but a psychological and moral one as well. Like Sartre's hero, Mathieu Delarue, he cannot find a commitment adequate to his freedom beyond the commitment to himself, the contents of his own mind, or to his art or métier. His inability to devote himself freely to a woman, to experience both sexual and "verbal" intercourse with her in a truly dialogic event (to use Buber's term), is but one expression of his failure of feeling and his impotence in the world. And impotent he remains whether he pursues no women or a hundred. Without the ability of the lover to love, the sexual acts in which he engages leave him dissatisfied and remorseful, filled only with words and dampened ardor, just as it leaves the woman unfulfilled and demeaned. As demonstrated by Singer's Asa Heshel (*The Family Moskat*) or the magician of Lublin, by Roth's Portnoy or Cahan's Levinsky, the sin against the family that the philanderer commits involves lying, coveting, stealing, and in a sense idolatry—in Portnoy's case an idolizing not of the woman but of his sole means of connecting himself to her.[2]

These ideas will be extended in the opening chapters. In the meantime I want to touch upon the relation between monologism and idolatry, a subject that, as I have said, introduces a new dimension of meaning to both terms. That the Mosaic injunction against graven images could in any way be relevant to life in this secular age seems most improbable, unless, that is, there is such a thing as aesthetic idolatry, the idolatry inherent in image-making and in the praise of objects or persons that we find in certain kinds of poetry. The so-called Objectivists, four Jewish poets whose work proved to be in the mainstream of modern American poetry, are a case in point.

Now, even though aesthetic idolatry is not religious idolatry, there is an instance in which they merge. Thus in Buber's theology a man who cannot speak to God, in dialogue, cannot speak *to*, only *at*, other men. Only men who cannot speak to God make idols, false gods, with whom there can be no communication, no interrelation, and therefore no awakening to oneself as a whole person. The idolater is perforce a monologist just as only a monologist can be an idolater.

Rest assured, I have no intention of accusing the Objectivists of being idolaters in the religious sense. But in the aesthetic sense, in the idea that Objectivism leads to an idealization, not to say apotheosis, of things in their gratuitous reality, that perhaps is something else again, especially since much of their poetry is so obscure as to be "noncommunicative." And to complicate the matter, the obscurity is not only often recognized by the poet, but regarded as an evil against which he struggles both literally and as a persona in his poems.

There is, finally, as I hope to show in part 4, a relation between monologism and anti-Semitism. The hero of Bruce Jay Friedman's novel *Stern* fantasizes engaging his anti-Semitic neighbor, whom he calls the "kike man," in a dialogue that aims at mutual understanding. No such conversation will take place, of course, because there can be no interchange between prejudice or obsession and its object. There is nothing Stern can say that will make the kike man change his mind (how could he and still be the kike man?). And there is nothing the kike man can say that will persuade Stern that he is what the kike man says he is or determines him to be.

The kike man, however, is not a wordsman and therefore

does not represent the more developed form of verbal anti-Semitism (or "anti-Semitic monologism"). Ezra Pound is—and in his dogmatism, which carries him from pedagogy, authentic teaching, to "pedagoguery," the propaganda of his pro-Fascist, anti-Semitic wartime radio speeches, he becomes the monologist in one of his most appalling forms. How Pound could fail to see the contradiction between his humanism and anti-Semitism, between his talent for high lyricism and his capacity for diatribe, are questions that have become the clichés of Pound criticism. And they are dangerous clichés in that they have often led to speculation that, in attempting in the name of objectivity to minimize, justify, or excuse Pound's transgressions, succeeds only in incriminating itself. Thus monologism begets monologism and the critic, instead of exonerating the Master, commits his sins.

If Hemingway's anti-Semitism pales before the enormity of Pound's, it still poses some crucial questions. Can anti-Semitism in a novel that might "otherwise" be considered a masterpiece be simply "overlooked" or rationalized as a fictive given? In other words can it be compartmentalized or is it like a drop of poison in the bloodstream? Specifically, is the achievement of *The Sun Also Rises,* Hemingway's first and no doubt most celebrated novel, merely "lessened," or is it wholly negated, by the treatment of Robert Cohn, a Jew whose bearing, conduct, and conversation earn him only the contempt of the hero, Jake Barnes, and his circle of friends? We ask, why is a Jew made the fool? Was Hemingway faithfully recording his relationship with Harold Loeb, the supposed real-life model of Cohn? Is Hemingway asking us to sympathize with Jake's view of Cohn?

As both narrator and participant in the events of the novel, Barnes is in full control of the information and the perspective from which it is given. And because we, as readers, have no way of testing or challenging his opinions or version of events, we are in effect listeners to a monologue, and the monologue is essentially Hemingway's. Even though he maintained that he wasn't Jake Barnes, Hemingway was clearly sympathetic to him, especially in the matter of Jake's attitude toward Cohn, which was analogous to Hemingway's attitude toward Loeb. What makes it possible for us to break into the monologue and gain a broader perspective on character and action is Loeb's version of himself, and the events on which the novel is based, in his autobiography, *The Way It Was*.

As a participant, Jake is shown chiefly through dialogue (in the conventional sense), but only in rare moments do we find him experiencing a true rapport with his partner—moments in which he is not thinking about his mutilation or else can joke about it. (Such dialogue often ends with a sharp reminder that brings him back to reality.) When speaking to Cohn, however, Jake always adopts a condescending tone and a kind of banter that keeps him firmly in control of the interchange, which is no genuine interchange at all but merely an exchange of monologues.

Monologism, which according to Bakhtin is the voice of order, stability, unity, and conformity, becomes the voice of tyranny; anti-Semitism, which begins with the slur, ends in persecution; persecution, which begins with the broken glass of a *Kristallnacht* ends in systematic mass murder. Finally, the language of authentic communication, the language of logos, turns into the language of mono-logos, the single-minded obsessive speech that destroys the humanity of the speaker just as he, verbally and literally, destroys that of the Jew. In the linguistics of the Holocaust, we are told by Lawrence Langer, dehumanization, which is the total assault upon mind, body, and soul, involves radical reduction of vocabulary, drastic alteration in the meanings of words, introduction of neologism, and other such devices to disorient the victim, in forcing him to accept his fate, as he is turned into an animal prior to being killed.

This was not exactly the situation of the Jew in Russia in 1911 as Bernard Malamud conceived of it in *The Fixer*, but

Malamud's vision of the Mendel Beiliss case is, with all its horrors, prophetic enough. Yakov Bok (Beiliss), falsely accused of ritual murder, suffers untold humiliations and torments as a prisoner of the state awaiting trial. Completely at the mercy of his tormentors for all communication, he is the victim par excellence of a totalitarian mono-logism in which violations of logic, distortion of fact, self-serving emotional appeals are all masked in the diction of rational or passionate argument in the effort to extract a confession.

They fail. The refusal to confess is Bok's only link with sanity, self-respect, and truth; finally, it is the only explanation for his survival. He does not survive because Jews survive and he is a Jew. He draws consistently upon no Jewish heritage and, in fact, is supported as much by a fragment of the New Testament as he is by what he has been able to obtain of the old. Carrying a grudge against God, he proclaims himself an atheist. No, Yakov Bok is not the representative Jew victimized by Russian persecution. He is the secular "little man" enmeshed in a bureaucratic spider's web and there is no transcendent meaning or justification for his suffering beyond that of the eternal struggle of the individual against a corrupt and noxious society.

In a moment of illumination Bok dedicates his suffering to all Russian Jews, who, he foresees, will be, if he confesses, the victims of pogroms. He therefore resolves to survive long enough to stand trial, where, he anticipates, the lies of the state will be exposed. That resolution is the basis of whatever good or "heroism" there is in the novel but it is not in any way a justification of suffering. As Bok will tell the Tsar in an imaginary discussion, the meaning of suffering is that suffering is meaningless. Always the practical man, the fixer experiences no mystical transformation that suffering, as a dark night of the soul, brings to the religious penitent, nor does he reach a tragic acceptance of God and His world. The one is for the *goyim*,

Introduction 11

the other for Jews. And Bok, as we have seen, is neither.

I realize that my insistence that Bok's experience is not tragic goes against the grain of Malamud criticism in general—Harap is representative when he asserts that Bok changes "from *shlemiel* to *mentsh.*" Indeed Harap is supported by Malamud himself whom he quotes as saying, " 'My story . . . is about imprisonment and the effort of liberation through the growth of a man's spirit.' "

Harap, however, cites, by way of contrast with his own, a quite different opinion of Bok, that of Philip Rahv, who argues that as a "victim pure and simple, Bok cannot attain the stature of a hero of a work of art." In this interpretation, which, Malamud's explicit statement to the contrary, I find the more logical of the two, Rahv explains that even though he is "transformed by a frenzied revolutionary imagination," Bok "remains inert as a character." My reasoning, however, is not at all Rahv's.

I am troubled most by the complication that if we accept the idea that Bok undergoes true spiritual growth, we accept with it the idea that there can be something positive in suffering in general and in anti-Semitism in particular. While this notion is the substance of tragedy, it comes perilously close to the view that suffering ennobles and that anti-Semitism, far from being an unmitigated evil, is God's way of testing Jews, building their character, making them worthy of their chosenness.

For those who believe, on the other hand, that there can be no justification for anti-Semitism, theological or characterological, Bok's imprisonment is not a test from which he emerges a hero, but a gratuitous, degrading ordeal that he survives. That he can call upon hidden strengths to do so is so much the better, but it doesn't make his experience one that has supposedly made a mensch of him and one that he should therefore be grateful for having had the opportunity to live through.

In the perspective of the Holocaust, Bok's story cannot

but have a meaning radically different from that when viewed without it. With horror, degradation, and murder raised to the six-millionth power, could distinctions such as hero and coward or dialogue and monologue or Thou and It or God's will and man's ever have any of the old meanings again?

Part One
Distance and Relation

1   Sartre and the Existential Jew

By "Existential Jew" I mean, simply, any Jew who, having abandoned monotheism and finding himself in moral anarchy, must create his own meaning and values and bear sole responsibility for his own conduct. This position is diametrically opposite that of the observant Jew, who, believing that he stands in intimate relation to the One, True, and Living God, dwells in a universe in which he finds meaning and authority beyond himself; that is, in a transcendent reality. Unlike Sartre's Antoine Roquentin, who must write a novel to impose order and fixity on an essentially "viscous" world, the Jew is guided by the Torah in his effort to interpret the Will of God and to understand men's place in the way of things.

I am aware that this distinction is, at this late date, scarcely more than a cliché; I refer to it because it is the main source of Martin Buber's quarrel with Sartre (along with Heidegger and Jung) in *Eclipse of God* and thereby is crucial to any inquiry into what is and what is not "existentialist" in Buber's philosophy. It also sheds light on Sartre's own version of the "Jewish Question" as it appears in *Anti-Semite and Jew*.

Now, even though it is not made explicit, one of the most important oppositions in Buber's view of the world and

1. Distance and Relation

Sartre's lies in their conceptions of the Other, and all that they imply about human relations—those of man to man, man to nature, and, finally, man to God. To Sartre, then, Other (*l'autrui*) means Alien; and even though he accepts Hegel's view that the self requires recognition from the Other in order to come to full awareness of itself ("I must obtain from the Other the *recognition* of my being"; "I find that being-for-others appears as a necessary condition for my being-for-myself"),[1] he still maintains that "conflict is the original meaning of being-for-others." Charging Hegel with "epistemological optimism," Sartre attempts to show that the Other can never be seen as anything but an object:

> The other is not a *for-itself* as he appears to me; I do not appear to myself as I am *for-the-other*. I am incapable of apprehending for myself the self which I am for the Other, just as I am incapable of apprehending on the basis of the *Other-as-object* which appears to me, what the Other is for himself. (242)

Radically individualistic when it comes to personal relations, Sartre is atomistic in his view of social relations. "No logical or epistemological optimism," he argues, "can cover the scandal of the plurality of consciousnesses," a plurality that founded on conflict can never be synthesized into a whole. Why is plurality a scandal and who is to blame? Sartre doesn't say, but we can guess: God has caused this scandal by his disappearance, taking with him all possibility of totality in the universe. Thus we find Sartre writing elsewhere: "Everything happens as if the world, man, and man-in-the-world succeeded in realizing only a missing God." And he makes the connection explicit:

> Everything happens therefore as if the in-itself and the for-itself were presented in a state of disintegration in relation to an ideal synthesis. Not that the integration has ever *taken place* but on the contrary precisely because it is always indicated and always impossible. (623)

Sartre and the Existential Jew

Just as the idea of God as *en sui causa*, a totality in which the for-itself and in-itself are fused into a true unity (the for-itself-in-itself), represents an ideal, so disillusion upon the loss of God reveals the world as a "disintegrated ensemble" or "detotalized totality." The implications of all this for social thought are clear: Sartre's world remains predicated on the individual, who, being irreducible to identity with any other person, cannot be synthesized into a community or social whole. Although this theory was not to be his last word on the subject, it remains an utterly logical part of Existentialism before Sartre's attempts to accommodate it to Marxism.[2] Finally, Sartre could say plainly and without equivocation, "So long as consciousnesses exist, the separation and conflict of consciousnesses will remain" (244).

In the dynamics of Existentialism, men are perpetually struggling to deprive the Other of his freedom (*liberté*) and thereby reduce him to an object. This occurs when the self *looks* in judgment at the Other, who, thus exposed to the gaze with which he is being categorized, feels his "transcendence being transcended" and burns with shame. Because the self or consciousness contemplates the world of Being (matter), it must be separate from it; it is therefore nonbeing or *Néant*, nothingness. One seeks to commit his freedom—exercise the wholly free will for whose acts he alone is responsible—and acquire an identity, but as Sartre's fiction vividly demonstrates, this is by no means an easy achievement. An easier way out is to accept evaluation or capture by the Other and to find security in the classification that he has made.

For the Jew, as Sartre has conceived of him, the primordial Other is the anti-Semite. Here, the former emerges as an undefinable "freedom," a nonbeing whose identity as a Jew is given him by the society; that is his "situation," outside of which he cannot exist as a Jew. It is, for example, essential to Jewish "nothingness" that there be no Jewish history in any normal sense of the word. Accordingly, Sartre tells us that a concrete historical community is basically *national* and *religious;* but the Jewish community ... has been deprived bit by bit of both these concrete characteristics. We may call it an abstract historical community. Its dispersion and political impotence forbid its having a *historic past.* If it is true ... that a community is historical to the degree that it remembers its history, then the Jewish community is the least historical of all, for it keeps a memory of nothing but a long martyrdom, that is, of a long passivity. (*Anti-Semite and Jew,* 91)

To repeat, nothing unifies this history-less community except a "common situation" among Jews, namely that they live in a community that "takes them for Jews." Sartre is referring here to the Jews of the Diaspora, especially those living in "Christian" countries and having as their goal participation in all aspects of the social and cultural life of the "host" nation; this would represent a level of assimilation perpetually denied them. "Thus the Jew remains the stranger, the intruder, the unassimilated man at the very heart of our society" (83).

Need it be said that Sartre has come very close to characterizing the Jew (just as he did Baudelaire and Genet) as Existential Man, an abstraction that while serving a metaphysical and social theory is reductionistic and misleading? The case of Roquentin, for example, even though metaphysical while that of the Jew is social, still can tell us much about Sartre's response to the Jewish Question. Roquentin, we recall, was a historian who after years of futile effort to complete the biography of an obscure eighteenth-century diplomat, the Marquis de Rollebon, loses all faith in the recoverability of the past: "Slow, lazy, sulky, the facts adapt themselves to the rigor of the order I wish to give them; but it remains outside them. I have the feeling of doing a work of pure imagination."

Roquentin's failure to impose order (necessity) on the facts of Rollebon's life (gratuity) and to recover the facts of his own past leaves him "forsaken in the present"—disoriented, alienated from the bourgeois world with all its certainties of time and place, position and destiny, and filled only with the sense of his own loss of essence, of the raw meaningless existence ebbing and flowing in both mind and body. This is, as I have suggested, the metaphysical and psychological analogue to the social situation of the Jew as Sartre perceives it.

There is, however, a complication that prevents us from embracing this view as the definitive explanation of Sartre's ideas on the subject. For following another stereotype, Sartre is convinced that the Jew is *sui generis* and that his situation is not to be compared to that of any other human group. What he is saying here is that the Jew can never stand for Everyman, mankind, or any other universal—including that of Existential Man.

Thus in his list of the traits exhibited by Jews ("whose life is nothing but a long flight from others and from [themselves]"), Sartre includes "uneasiness"—Jewish uneasiness, as he carefully specifies. This is not, we learn, the "anxiety that moves us to a consideration of the condition of modern man." Metaphysics is something permitted only to those in society who are certain of their position, "free from the fears that assail oppressed minorities and classes." In other words, only the bourgeois oligarchy, wrapped in the certitudes of its right to command, "dares" to view man in cosmic or universalist terms. The Jew, as the very opposite of the bourgeois leader, never sure of his position or his possessions . . . his situation, his power, and even his right to live—may be placed in jeopardy from one moment to the next" (132).

Even though in one sense he may possess the very traits exhibited by a Roquentin, and a similar situation, alienation from both the "serious" bourgeois world and the physical universe, the Jew engages in a struggle that is completely limited to its psychological and social content and has no transcendent significance. Everything he does pertains to himself alone. For not only is "uneasiness" not *angoisse,* but reason is not reason, tact is not tact, and the desire for money is more than the lust for profit. No matter how closely they resemble their counterparts in the serious world, these traits are to be interpreted as the means by which the "inauthentic" Jew tries to escape from his situation into assimilation, to acquire the universalist character that transcends particular Jewishness, Jewishness being that nonexistent essence defined and detected only by a hostile society.

Terms like authentic and inauthentic are, we recall, associated with the theory of *mauvais foi,* an intricate and ambiguous notion that among other things defines the attempt to be what one is not. Jews would seem to fit this classification perfectly, and in fact "authentic" and "inauthentic" bring much of their existential import to the argument: thus, as we have seen, there are inauthentic Jews, obsessed with escaping from what they are (Jews-in-situation) to what they are not (man-in-the-world); and there are authentic Jews, whose authenticity consists in choosing to be what they are—but what they are, in fact, turns out to be like nothing that is:

> The authentic Jew abandons the myth of the universal man; he knows himself and wills himself into history as a historic and damned creature; he ceases to run away from himself and to be ashamed of his own kind. He understands that society is bad.... He knows that he is one who stands apart, untouchable, scorned, proscribed—and it is as such that he asserts his being.... he accepts the obligation to live in a situation that is defined precisely by the fact that it is unlivable; he derives pride from his humiliation. (136–37)

Sartre concludes that the authentic Jew, possessing none of the characteristics of the inauthentic Jew, "is what he makes himself, *that is all that can be said.*"

He's wrong: not only is there more to be said, but everything remains to be said. This description is specious in a sense that can't be explained away by the existential logic that supposedly produced it. To begin with, authenticity, for Sartre, means that the Jew accept the situation that the anti-Semite has created for him. He is asked to live an unlivable condition and derive pride from humiliation; he must find his identity in the nonidentity of the pariah. Insofar as it implicitly confirms the anti-Semitic shibboleth that the Jews are not and can never be "one of us," that the Jew is not only *an* alien but alien from the human race, and that his authenticity depends upon his recognition of this reality, this formulation is dangerously misleading.

The truth is that Sartre's faith in existential principles, specifically in the ones that decree consciousness to be nonbeing or negation, has in this case been maintained at heavy cost. In the abstract, all mankind is superfluous (*de trop*), and there being no Creator there can be no created human nature; but what we can accept as part of an ontological and epistemological discussion, we cannot accept when applied to a moral, psychological, and social one, especially when it is apparent that the ethnic group involved is being regarded not as representative Existential Man but as an aberrant and eccentric phenomenon.

Sartre's position on Jewish authenticity is indefensible; it is so because he ignores the positive values and ideals associated with Judaism in general and with the Jew's vision of himself.[3] If the Jew in the Diaspora has no history, he does quite obviously have a tradition and heritage that links him to the past. He may be, like Roquentin, a pariah in Christian-bourgeois society, but he is not, unlike Roquentin, "forsaken in the present." In fact, that is precisely one of his chief problems. (I. B. Singer, for example, devotes several hundred pages in three major novels to the resistance of Polish Jews to entering the twentieth century.) Inhabiting a world that is becoming increasingly "decentered," Roquentin is beset by pure, meaningless existence, objectified as a viscous substance that induces both a literal and spiritual nausea. This is not the experience of

1. Distance and Relation

the Jew, who, whatever he suffers, however he sins, is drawn to the supreme Center of all things. All Jews, authentic or inauthentic, Polish or American, shtetl-livers or urban dwellers, utter "Shma yisroel adonoi elohenu adonoi echud" (Hear, O Israel, the Lord our God, the Lord is One!). Singer believes that the Jews (chiefly the Hasidim) have a faith that more than compensates for "the memory of a long martyrdom . . . of a long passivity" that Sartre argues is all the Jews in the Diaspora have of "history":

> [The Jews] had been driven out of Russia, were the victims of pogroms, writers had vilified them, called them parasites; anti-Semites had manufactured false accusations against them. But instead of becoming degenerate, sinking into melancholy, drunkenness, and immorality—they celebrated, recited the Psalms, rejoiced with happiness that could come only from the soul. No one here was in despair over pogroms, as were the Jewish intelligentsia all over Russia. They placed their faith in God, not in man, evolution, or revolution. (*The Estate*, 336)

Describing the authentic Jew, Sartre may have shown what can be done with existential logic, but he didn't have anything to say about Judaism. Like the "inauthentic Jew," the authentic one is but an ensemble of negations, the response to an unfavorable milieu and situation. Now what reason would there be for the observant Jew to accept the fate of social scorn, alienation, and humiliation were it not in the belief that he is serving God? Since God is dead, Sartre can establish his ideal only in terms of an abstract and demeaning condition in which the Jew, who is what he is because of his faith in a certain relationship with God, is asked to be what he is and suffer what he does only in the interests of an authenticity or good faith that has no meaning beyond itself.

The Hasids, says a character in Singer, are "the real Jews, the Jews who live with God." And this is exactly what makes martyrdom and passivity two different things and transforms the Jew from a mere negation upon whom things are imposed into a figure of affirmation with an identity and an existence dependent on no one but himself and his God. He has the free will to choose between good and evil but at the same time must interpret and comprehend the will of deity that gives human will its meaning and raises man above the pagan, who can know only strife and violence. What is particularly ironic in this conception is that logically Sartre is bound to condemn the authentic Jew's faith in God in that the very quality that makes him a Jew is an example of *mauvais foi* since it represents a blindness to the real nature of existence (Godless).

We are not surprised to find in Sartre's portrait of the anti-Semite in the novella called *The Childhood of a Leader (L'Enfance d'un chef)*, as well as in the first half of *Anti-Semite and Jew*, a mirror image to that of the Jew. And that is why it is ultimately unacceptable. The story of Lucien Fleurie is the story of the "characterless" man, the man who feels himself to be a nothing, essenceless, without being—whose sense of self is determined by the opinion of others or by what he takes to be the opinion of others. His struggle is the familiar one of the weak character in an existential world, that of acquiring position and place in "serious" bourgeois society with all its certitudes, rights, and "moral health." Lucien's childhood is an endless round of role-playing in which he continually questions what really and truly exists. Indulged and pampered, he grows up dandified and narcissistic, a *deraciné*, who, after encounters with Freudianism, Unanimism, Surrealism, and pederasty, joins the Camelots, a reactionary youth group, and becomes a rabid anti-Semite.

The Camelots offer him a character and a destiny, a means of escaping the "inexhaustible gossip of his conscience," a method of defining and appreciating himself. Thus it is not Jew-hating in itself that motivates him, but rather the desire to be known as a Jew-hater, the fulfillment of which brings respectability and all the privileges that go with membership in the middle class. In short, Lucien is an inauthentic anti-Semite, an actor playing a role before others. His real sin is that of vanity and if any trait lends consistency to his personality it is this one. Because this is the case, because a penchant for theatricality and a craving for attention underlie all his behavior, we cannot take him seriously. I do not deny that he may well represent a kind of anti-Semite, the way the inauthentic Jew represents a kind of Jew, but as such he is little more than a caricature, just as the Jews he encounters are caricatures, weak shadowy figures who offer little resistance or masochistically invite attack by jeering their tormentors. Seeing them only through Lucien's eyes, how can we possibly think of them as actual human beings and not mere phantoms of the existential imagination?

Anti-Semitism, of course, has many forms and Sartre cannot be faulted for his choice even though it is exotic. Still, considering the state of the Jews at the end of World War II, he might have tried deeper and more perilous waters where the real thing lurked. The truth is, I suspect, that Sartre's interest in the Jewish Question was limited. At least the world he has depicted in his most important literary endeavor, *Chemins de la liberté*, dominated though it might be by multiple consciousnesses in constant strife and anxiety, is, in its major characters, *Judenfrei*.

Of his three classifications, that of the "inauthentic Jew" is, without doubt, Sartre's most provocative, if not provoking. But even here in this portrait of the Jew, single-minded and obsessed in his attempt to assimilate into the country in which he lives, there is an element of sketchiness and oversimplification. No provision exists for the Jew trying to reconcile religious belief and national identity—the kind of Jew who is probably in the majority in Western society. If Sartre's category is to have any genuine significance beyond the love of wordplay, rhetoric, and paradox, it is because it offers us an excellent point of departure for understanding the kind of Jew that appears most frequently in fiction—both comic and serious. The Jew who has simultaneously assimilated and continues to observe the ceremonies and rituals as faith in God requires is not of great dramatic interest. More so is the fictitious Authentic Jew, of whom Sartre asks martyrdom not because it is the outcome of serving God but because it is an inevitable part of his situation and to recognize it is to act in *bon foi*.

The term "Inauthentic Jew," insofar as it is normative as well as descriptive, carries an opprobrium with it that leads to caricature rather than realistic portrayal. The idea of self-hatred that underlies this image is itself, I believe, equally an exaggeration and more suited to melodrama than to philosophic analysis.

When the Jew ceases to believe in God and to follow His Law, he finds himself in an existential situation; having abandoned faith in a transcendent reality as a source of value and a guide to conduct, he becomes aware of his own freedom of choice and moral independence and suffers the anxiety and sense of guilt that accompanies them. That enlightenment is a mixed blessing, bringing intellectual confusion as well as liberation, and moral disintegration as well as release, is a fundamental theme in Singer and, indeed, the "Existential Jew"—the Jew who no longer a monotheist is faced with finding meaning and value on his own—appears throughout Jewish fiction. Shrouded in ambiguity, the existential world offers no possibility of a definitive and permanently fulfilling commitment of one's freedom or the exercise of one's "self-will" in a consistently purposeful manner, just as it can offer no ultimate revelation.

It has not been my intention to present yet another abstraction of the Jew, accompanied as it is by a label that has long since been a cliché. But the term and the basic principles it signifies do retain a certain usefulness as a point of departure for understanding another mode of thought—one that will bring us closer to the heart of the subject.

2 Buber and the Dialogical Jew

Sartre could have accused Martin Buber of committing the same sin as that committed by Hegel and Heidegger—namely, ontological and epistemological optimism. Buber, in his turn, accused Sartre of "wretched fatalism." Both, of course, are correct though irrelevant. The epithets become meaningless just as soon as we recall that Sartre spent his later years trying to build a positive superstructure on the foundation of existential nihilism and conversely Buber speculated on the inevitable decline of his ideal "Thou" into an "It" or object, a phenomenon that the existentialist might well understand. Still, we become cognizant of similarities to all the more appreciate differences. Sartre defines human experience in terms of competition and seeks a means of qualifying that judgment; Buber defines human experience in terms of cooperation but recognizes an existential dimension in which conflict and exploitation are paramount.

"Thou," as we shall see presently, is the primordial word by which men come together in a relationship or meeting—a "dialogic event"—in which true communication occurs and in the full awareness of himself as a complete human being, a man senses the other as a "presence." "Complete human being" means here that one is not limited in his perception and judgment to a single faculty, but responds with his whole being, something that is greater than the sum of its parts, such as intellect, feeling, and imagination, and thereby transcends what we commonly call experience. How precisely this view is the diametrical opposite of the existential view is made clear in Buber's assertion that

> Sartre regards the walls between the partners in a conversation as simply impassable. For him it is inevitable human destiny that a man has directly to do only with himself and his own affairs. The inner existence of the other is his own concern, not mine; there is no direct relation with the other, nor can there be. (*Knowledge of Man,* 79)

Whereas in Sartre the look signifies the attempt to turn the Other into an object, in Buber

> the one who lives from his being looks at the other just as one looks at someone with whom he has personal dealings. . . . he produces a look which is meant to have . . . the effect of a spontaneous utterance—not only the utterance of a psychical event supposed to be taking place at that very moment, but also . . . the reflection of a personal life of such-and-such a kind. (76)

"Spontaneous utterance," the basis of true dialogue, is the response of the "whole man" and involves the "making present" of the other. What this means specifically is that in *relation* a man "imagines the real," becomes aware of what "another man is at this very moment wishing, feeling, perceiving, thinking, and not as a *detached content,* but in his very reality, that is, as a living process in this man." A relation is "ontologically complete" only when the other knows that he is made present by me in his self and when this knowledge "induces the process of his inmost self-becoming." Growth of the self, Buber argues, "is accomplished not in man's relation to himself, but in the relation between one and the other . . . together with the mutuality of acceptance, of affirmation and confirmation."

Now, in the empirical or existential world—the world of existents, objects, matter—men, as well as things are seen as a "detached content"; they "live round about us as components of the independent world over against us." This is what Buber means by "distance," the act of separating oneself from objects and men and thereby establishing them in their independence and otherness. Man must distance himself to use and experience things and to reduce other men to objects; that one is an object for the other, says Buber, is, according to the existentialists, the "basic factor between men" (74). The basic factor for Buber is that one can also make the other a partner in a living dialogical event, and that entails their transfiguration from component into whole and that of their relation from I-It to I-Thou.[1] It also means the transformation of their conversation from monologue into dialogue, from the cacophony of everyday chatter and babble, in which one is speaking only to himself, into *Logos,* the Heraclitean Word that is "common to all" and thus signifies community and communication. Thus Buber: "When Heraclitus says of the Logos . . . that it is common, he thereby asserts that all men in the eternal originality of their spoken intercourse with one another have a share in the consummation of this indwelling" (90).

Such is Buber's interpretation of the fragment of Heraclitus, discussed briefly in the introduction. Buber sees here support for his belief that language is a thoroughly social phenomenon—that it has no existence even in the individual man engaged in thought, who is, in effect, his own listener. Monologue, we are told, cannot be authentic conversation because it lacks the other person and therefore the tension of surprise. Only with a genuine partner does language come into being as the spoken word and only then are questions and answers real ones. The decisive use of language involves one's coming to an understanding with others about situations, not just naming objects (116). Thus for Buber an ideal language exists in the region "between" two men in actual dialogue, a conversation, based on sincerity and trust, in which agreement or disagreement is irrelevant and what matters is that each conversant speak from his whole self:

> where the dialogue is fulfilled in its being, between partners who have turned to one another in truth, who express themselves without reserve and are free of the desire for semblance, there is brought into being a memorable common fruitfulness which is to be found nowhere else. (86)

Fulfilled by social action in an authentic community, the whole man stands in contradistinction to the falsely free man who pursues his own goals and remains alienated and rootless in a collectivity that is mere composite and not an integrated organism.

In the fragmented world, man lives the "life of monologue" where encounter, not meeting, prevails. Only a part of the person speaks; only a fragment of the self is conscious as the speaker attempts to persuade or inform, or is simply caught up in his own rhetoric. In solipsism, a fragment taking itself as a whole, the speaker rants, babbles, or raves around an obsession and has no regard for the listener's responses. The listener becomes an object (a sounding board), an "it" that exists outside the speaker but whose replies are distorted into meanings that best suit the speaker's delusions.

When the dialogic event goes beyond personal relations, those who have learned how to say "Thou" can say "We," the true pronoun for communality. As "We," says Buber, "man has not only experiences with others and with himself . . . but has constructed and developed a world out of [these experiences]." We've already seen that according to Sartre the Jews have no "community of interests" or "community of beliefs." The "sole tie that binds them," he argues, "is the hostility and disdain of the societies that surround the Jew" (*Anti-Semite and Jew*, 91). (In other words, anti-Semitism is all that makes a Jew a Jew!) If he can later say that the Jew is the social man par excellence, he means it in no positive sense: it is only "because the Jew's torment is social." "Society, not the decree of God . . . has made him a Jew and brought the Jewish problem into being" (134).

But for Buber, and Judaism in general, it is precisely the decree of God that makes Jews Jewish—or, if not decree of, then dialogue with, God, fellow Jews, and ideally the whole "interhuman" world. There is no little irony in the fact that the Jews, whose whole conception of themselves is socially oriented, should be characterized as socially nonexistent by a philosopher whose view of man is radically individualistic and whose social thought has turned out to be the least original part of his doctrine.

It is his conception of the ethical, as well as methodological, dimensions of dialogue that makes Buber a philosopher of unusual interest to modern and postmodern literature. Although I shall make no attempt to prove any direct influence of Buber on Jewish literature, the proximity of his ideas to certain aspects of Hasidism may very well have made him more directly influential than I have given him credit for. My only claim is that an I-Thou perspective, very broadly interpreted, is of great value in the criticism of fiction and drama, especially but not exclusively, Jewish-American, comic no less than melodramatic or tragic. Whatever the rarity of the I-Thou moment, that ultimate moment of turning to a partner in genuine dialogue to reveal oneself and be revealed to by the Other, the I-It moment, upon which the world turns, is as common as everyday reality and often as fit a subject for irony or satire. Here, where all communication has broken down, the monologist prevails: speakers, pursuing their own discourse, are wholly insensitive to the presence of the Other, whose responses have a "mono-logic" of their own or else cease altogether. Thus the listener becomes the It in an I-It relation.

The way one addresses another is an indication of one's character and moral situation. That, I believe, is the most important principle the literary critic can take from Buber. I say this not only by way of summing up, but also by way of warning. We cannot be too sensitive to the twin perils of reducing a literary work to theology or philosophy and, conversely, simplifying or distorting the latter in the attempt to demonstrate its literary relevance. The heights of abstraction to which Buber carries the I-Thou relation would be irrelevant to the very novels that best demonstrate its simpler, broader meaning as a moment of true intimacy, sincerity, unselfishness, understanding, communication, fulfillment. And so with the I-It, which has complexities we need not go into if the fiction is to retain its own vitality and significance.

That having been said, we bring forth an abstraction of our own. The Dialogical Jew, like Sartre's Authentic Jew, is a platonic idea, the image of an ideal; but where the latter is founded upon negation and is empty of content, the former possesses a power of speech and communication that bespeaks the depth of his character. Because he depends not upon the Other but upon God for his identity or definition of being, he has a natural transcendence that cannot be transcended. Specifically, as a Jew, he derives his ultimate significance from the relations between Moses and God, partners in dialogue just as they are partners to a covenant. God speaks to man and man to God, and when man listens, so does God. (I venture to say that one of Moses' greatest moments in his relationship to God appears in the golden calf episode, when the Almighty, ready to vent his wrath on the Israelites for having betrayed him, not only listens to what man says but actually is persuaded to change his mind; "And the Lord repented of the evil which he thought to do unto his people." God listens because Moses is *present* to Him; he is not only *there* physically but, since he has proved his faith—because he himself has demonstrated his understanding of God's will by ordering the idolaters to be slain—he is there ethically and spiritually in his whole person.)

Our major concern, however, is with the unredeemed counterpart to the "Dialogical Jew," and that is the Jew who, no longer able to find completion in God, speaks only to himself or to those whom he would exploit. Having no transcendent or coherent set of values that will enable him to "make a statement" or "take a stand" or, in effect, to "turn to a Presence" that can give him moral guidance, the Monological Jew reveals in every utterance the egocentric life that he must endure. Although he may defend the ideals of the Enlightenment, they are not enough to make life meaningful and they eventually leave him bored, confused, and apathetic, a state he often flees by committing adultery or indulging in whatever other forms of dissipation suit his personality.

This is, of course, a composite view, a schema that the actual fictional character will incarnate and particularize so that the problems he represents will take on their full meaning and make their greatest dramatic impression on the reader. At the risk of belaboring the point, I must emphasize that, whatever appearances, I am not using the expression "Monological Jew" in any technical sense. I am, in short, exchanging precision for flexibility and, I imagine, denotation for connotation or literal statement for metaphor. Thus, the Monological Jew may well prove to be a chimera or figment. If we are fortunate, he may also turn out to be a Proteus who at least once in a while can be caught in a revealing position.

Part Two
The Monological Jew in Fiction

3 Stern's Silent Monologue

Continually in flight from his "Jewishness," or at least the kind of Jewishness that prevents him from blending into the gentile culture around him, Stern, the antihero of Bruce Jay Friedman's minor masterpiece, is a chronic rationalizer and fantasist, driven by paranoia, anxiety, and a general sense of guilt. He is obsessed with the "kike man," an anti-Semitic neighbor who insulted his wife and is reported to have "seen" her when he pushed her down and, not having underwear on, she was exposed to view. This is only the most nagging in a series of daily incidents and encounters with the parade of eccentrics and grotesques that populate his world. Eventually, Stern develops an ulcer that sends him to a nursing home and later to a showdown with his arch-antagonist.

On the face of it, Stern seems to answer Sartre's description of the "inauthentic" Jew—but with two exceptions. He is not an abstraction, with a merely schematic reality, but a fictional character who is drawn in detail and reveals a high degree of complexity.[1] Equally important is that his flight from Jewishness does not necessarily mean a flight from being Jewish. Although he accepts himself as a Jew only insofar as he can elicit the admiration and respect of the *goyim*, the Others, who determine his status in the world, he will not convert to Christianity, no matter what his attitude toward his Jewish heritage.

The only trouble is that Stern has no meaningful Jewish heritage. Sporadically and during high holy days, he does attend *shul,* but we learn that "there was little God to his religion" and that when he went away to college, "even the trappings fell away" (*Stern,* 43). " 'I don't care much about being a Jew,' " he announces at this time. He can say this because he has almost no idea of what being a Jew is like. Taken as a child to holiday services, he stands in ignorance "among bowing, groaning men who wore brilliantly embroidered shawls." Even after three years of Hebrew school, he finds that he cannot fit in, that his own bowing and groaning is merely theatrical, and that he remains "a loner among the chanting sufferers at synagogues" (43).

The experience proves to be typical. Stern learns how to read Hebrew aloud at a "mile-a-minute clip," but, as far as comprehension went, he "might as well have been performing in Swahili or Urdu" (44). "No great religious traditions were handed down to Stern by his ... father," Friedman writes, and there follows an account of the Passover "seder" (ritual dinner), attended by the whole family, that ends in a shouting match and ill feeling. Comic though it may be, with its colorfully vociferous eccentrics, this episode records a disintegrated family practicing an all but meaningless religion.[2] What should have been a *meeting* (in Buber's sense) is nothing more than a gathering of articulate, though hopelessly monological, solipsists, who speak a low comic rhetoric that is a moral opposite to the Heraclitean Logos and the dialogue through which it is expressed.

A novel of caricature can present only an absurd universe and an absurd view of human relations. The Judaism that Stern knows—the Judaism that in fact has made him— never rises above this profane level. A gagster who delights in punning, his father "has great fun with such phrases as 'orange Jews' and 'grapefruit Jews,' " and Stern, living in a

Jewish boarding house while at college, shows that the apple does not fall far from the tree:

> There grew up among the three [roommates] a jargon and patter, all of which hinged on Jewishness. . . . Stern might make a remark about the weather, to which [one roommate] would say, "How Jewish of you to say that." If Stern were to utter a pronouncement of any kind, [another roommate] would invariably retort: "Said with characteristic Jewishness." (50–51)

Far from being speech-with-meaning, this word is, to use Sartre's term, a "phrase-object," which in this context is a word that does no more than elicit an aesthetic response—that is, conveys a sensation that is basically inexpressible. But to call "Jewishness" a phrase-object is to lend the usage of this term a dignity it does not have. Potentially an in-group word with the power of conveying a sense of unity, it suffers a hollow repetition that has nothing more than a sophomoric amusement value. The camaraderie it represents turns out to be thin and the habit a bad one when other, more offensive, terms are introduced as names and the group eventually dissolves with suppressed ill feeling.

During the war, Stern serves in the Air Force as a nonflying officer; he feels guilty about his status and the idea of Jewishness, never far from his mind, comes up again when he associates nonflying with it,

> as though flying were a golden, crew cut, gentile thing while Jewishness was a cautious and scholarly quality that crept into engines and prevented planes from lurching off the ground with recklessness. (54)

When he is airsick in a general's private plane, he speaks of "cowardly Jewish vomit staining the golden aircraft." Actually, this is what Stern imagines the crew to be thinking

38   2. The Monological Jew in Fiction

as they file off the plane past him, but he obviously concurs in the sentiment.

In any case, this part of the novel has been leading up, all the time, to Stern's great moment when on leave he drifts into a local temple and, mistaken for a flying hero, creates a sensation among the congregation and its rabbi, who not only insist that he conduct the religious ceremonies, but wine-and-dine him and see that all his appetites are satisfied:

> Wasn't it wonderful. A Jewish boy. A fighter. A man who had shot down planes. Yet when there's a holiday he puts on a tallith and with such sweetness comes to sit in synagogues. And did you see him pray? Even in a uniform he reads so beautifully. Stern loved it, and when they shot him glances, he responded with religious groans and dipping bows and as much humility as he could summon. (56)

The sheer theatricality on both sides should have been enough to have made a shambles of the service and to have dissipated whatever religious emotion had existed among the worshippers.[3] This episode would be analogous to that of the seder were it not for the additional element of imposture on which it is based. Ironically, Stern, who cannot see himself as an authentic Air Force officer (which he is), is able to impersonate an officer and a hero (which he is not) without any qualms or self-consciousness, a curious variation on the theme of *mauvais foi*. All of Stern's contact with Judaism is of this kind. He is always a performer, never a true believer:

> On the day of the Bar Mitzvah, Stern [sang] the Haftarah flawlessly and his mother afterward said, "You had some voice. I could have fainted."
> "Yes," said the Haftarah coach. "But there was too much crooning." (45)

Stern's response to Judaism and Jewishness, however, is really no different from his usual response to any prob-

Stern's Silent Monologue 39

lematic situation, which rarely fails to produce a fantasy expressed in the rhetoric of a heated, highly theatrical imagination fueled by paranoia—the more trivial the incident the more caricatured the result. In one such episode Stern is sitting at a drugstore counter watching the owner (Doroff) flirting with an attractive woman he himself covets. Doroff is playing the one-upmanship game with specialty restaurants (Where do you "gopher" Chinese?) to Stern's increasing disgust:

> He wanted to holler out *"Where do you gopher shit?"* but he was certain Doroff would call out a number, sixty-two, and a drugstore plan would go into operation in which all eight countermen would loyally spring over the grill and trap Stern against the paperback books, hitting him in the stomach a few times and then holding him for a paid-off patrolman (69).

Now, this fantasy, expressed through a characteristically exaggerated rhetoric, has only one listener, Stern himself. Stern always *wants to* say, wants to cry out, but never does, being barred by cowardice or good sense or whatever it is that keeps him from entering into authentic relationships with others. And he is justified insofar as the others, preoccupied with turning their own feelings into theater through a rhetoric of their own, will not listen to him anyway. (Since in fantasy the actual object or "It" is never engaged, this relation might better be called an I-I, rather than an I-It, for we have here passed beyond monologue to arrive at "soliloquy," the natural mode of solipsism.)[4]

Stern's situation becomes critical when he learns that he has an ulcer, an affliction that he blames on the kike man. It leads to a nervous breakdown in which his desperation to talk to someone becomes acute and he accosts both friends and strangers pleading for a hearing. He finds no relief in any area of social life—not in his family, job with an advertising agency, or military service. In other words, no aspect of his waking (or sleeping) life provides him with a partner-in-dialogue. Here, for example, is a classical non-conversation between Stern and his friend, a black painter who speaks well and at length about his own achievements:

> The next time Battleby paused for breath, Stern said, "I don't feel so good. I've got to go away for a while. Look, we never talk, but I've got to talk to someone. Something happened to me out where I live. A guy did this to me because I'm Jewish. You probably run into a lot of Negro things. We never talked about stuff like this before, but I thought we could now."
> Battleby fidgeted on his chair and gulped for air, blinking at Stern incredulously, as if to say, "You don't understand. The conversation is about me. I talk about things that have happened to me, and I don't get into other things."
> Battleby said: "I've got some crucifixion oils I'd love for you to see. Real giant things with a powerful religious quality. I don't see how I was able to come up with them."
> "No, I mean it," Stern said. "I have to talk to someone."
> (78–79)

Hopelessly monological, Battleby eventually gives some cryptic advice that shows no real comprehension or compassion and upon his abrupt departure, Stern's ulcer awakens "angry, red-eyed, and vengeance-seeking." Whether his failure to achieve an I-Thou dialogue with Battleby lay with the inadequacy of Stern's rhetoric and the general weakness of his character or with Battleby's monologism is impossible to tell. Perhaps both can be blamed. Still, we are aware that for all his desire to enter into authentic dialogue, Stern will be thwarted by his own instincts for theater and by his rationalizing logic.

Instead of leading to an insight into himself and others, and of realizing himself as a whole human being, Stern's emotions are a caricature that reduces a potentially ideal relationship to farce. In one of his more appalling day-

Stern's Silent Monologue 41

dreams, for example, he imagines how he would respond to the kike man's being afflicted with a lower-back injury:

> Stern saw himself running over with extended hand and showing the man that he would not take advantage of him, that he would not fight him in his weakened condition, that Jews can forgive. He wanted opportunities to demonstrate that Jews are magnanimous, that Jews are sweet and hold no grudges. (98)

If this passage seems to express the Christian imperative "Love thine enemy," so much the worse for Christianity. But it doesn't. Nor does it reflect anything in Buber's philosophy, even though Stern is here trying to open a dialogue with the kike man. Were Stern motivated by truly charitable feelings, he would be merely excessive and ignorant, if there is any truth to Sartre's view that the anti-Semite can never change his mind about the Jew no matter what he is, says, or does.

But this fantasy is not motivated by benevolence; it is motivated by cowardice and a total inability to face reality. We know—as Friedman knows—that Stern will never get satisfaction from the kike man by words alone, that it is going to be through violence or not at all that he will find relief. And Stern knows it too; that is why he has an ulcer.

If Stern's benevolence is suspect, his protective instincts have the same histrionic or absurd quality that mark the feelings of the low comic figure in general, or would if they were actually demonstrated and not merely "thought about": "Stern felt sorry for Feldner in his bathrobe, a man whose shoulders had grown sad from so many disappointments, and wanted to hug him to make him feel better" (112). He has associated Feldner, a fellow patient in the nursing home, with his mother, who had worn old bathrobes into the street to protest her low clothing allowance from his father: "Now Stern wanted to embrace Feldner as though to make it up to his mother for turning his back

2. The Monological Jew in Fiction

on her saintlike bathrobed street marches" (112). So it happens that not even an exaggerated tenderness but a sense of guilt lies behind his wish. And knowing what his mother, another wordsman and solipsist with whom he has never had a "Thou" conversation, was like, we cannot help questioning the appropriateness of even this, mostly self-oriented, emotion.

Stern's adventures in the nursing home can bring no more than temporary satisfaction. An eccentric among grotesques, he enjoys what he thinks is camaraderie with the Greek, a hood, who, having lost a leg in a street fight, is confined to a wheel chair, and the "blond boy," a manic-depressive given to mock-violence:

> ... they were comrades of a sort and he was glad to be with them ... to be running and bellowing to the sky at their sides; he was glad their lives were tangled up together. It was so much better than being a lone Jew stranded on a far-off street, your exit blocked by a heavy-armed kike hater in a veteran's jacket. (124)

This is sincere enough, though Stern is deluded if he thinks the camaraderie is anything more than bare toleration. He later gets involved with a Puerto Rican girl, over whom the blond boy has asserted rights, but neither this experience nor the whole nursing home episode solves anything. Cured of his ulcer, Stern returns home to a nervous breakdown in which his frenetic search for a Listener leads him to accost women in the street and hold long fruitless conversations on the telephone with his mother and sister. Even though the search fails, the novel concludes with a moment of family intimacy that begins with the theatrical but ends with what seems to be genuine or at least motivated by the right reasons:

> [Stern] said, "I feel like doing some hugging," and knelt beside the sleeping boy.... His wife was at the door and Stern said, "I want you in here, too." She came over, and it

> Stern said, "I want you in here, too." She came over, and it occurred to him that he would like to try something a little theatrical, just kneel there quietly with his arms protectively draped around his wife and child. He tried it and wound up holding them a fraction longer than he'd intended. (159)

Stern's showdown with the kike man having left him with nothing more serious than a torn ear and a brief cessation of fear, that "fraction longer than he intended" holds the key to his salvation as a human being. Here, if the episode is indeed authentic and not mere sentiment or theater, a few seconds of silence is a whole dialogue.

Stern inhabits a world both intensely linguistic, speech being the chief mode of encounter and response, and intensely moral, Jewishness being the source of values by which conscience and self-consciousness make themselves felt. It is also a world that, populated mostly by eccentrics and grotesques, is comic throughout. Friedman, for instance, like other writers in the Jewish renaissance of the sixties, is not interested in getting behind his characters to expose the social or economic conditions that made them what they are, and it would be superfluous, if not irrelevant, to seek causes of behavior and personality, say, in class warfare or even the events of childhood. The characters are what they speak and if their monologism is directly proportional to their egocentricity, it is also on another level an index to the linguistic mastery of their creator. On the other hand, the genius of the comic novelist rarely, if ever, transcends the I-It relation. It is no accident that *Stern* concludes with a gesture and silence—and just as well that it does.

4 The Tenants of Moonbloooo-ooo

When the final *m* in Moonbloom's name, inscribed on the window of his realty office, is gradually scraped away, all the *o*'s come bubbling out in an endless flow, crooning an "infinite note of ache and joy." This fanciful "liberation of the word" marks that of Norman Moonbloom himself, who, feeling born again, is "thrilled . . . with his own endlessness." Thus Edward Wallant's novel, *The Tenants of Moonbloom,* virtually a comic anatomy of monologism in a dilapidated culture, concludes on a high note. There may be only a few instances in the novel of dialogue achieved, but they at least suggest that there is some kind of release from the monological life in which the *o*'s are bound up in a fixed name just as the bearer of that name is bound up in a routine of rent collection.

Having attended more than a dozen colleges and universities, at which he majored in a different subject each time, Moonbloom holds no degrees and pursues no career. Rather he seems to be languishing in a job given to him by his brother Irwin, a wealthy investor. The job is agent or manager of four run-down apartment houses in Manhattan. His chief function, in addition to collecting rent, is listening to complaints, although he is by no means obligated to do anything about them. And, in fact, he doesn't do much more than report them to the harried superintendent and to his brother.

Now, Moonbloom is the very image of the isolated man wholly separated from reality as it is observed in the normal world. As he walks, "his face show[s] no awareness of all the thousands of people around him because he traveled in an eggshell through which came only subdued light and muffled sound" (*Tenants*, 9). And in the same way, "he kept to a small circumference of sensation now, having experienced nothing that compensates for the discomfort of sensation" (43).

Insofar as they keep him from becoming involved with his clients, these limitations make Moonbloom a competent rent collector. But because he has no sympathy for the petty problems that daily besiege them, or the anguish that they belie, his tenants, each from his own point of view and for his own reasons, consider him cold, unfeeling, and only half-alive. As one tenant puts it, " 'Hey . . . I feel pain, I'm full of sensation. I've got an idea that you could watch a murder committed and just smile your goofy little shit-eating smile. You're like a body under water' " (45).

Like Stern, Moonbloom is an eccentric in a world of grotesques, a fictive world in which one is what one speaks and conversation is the measure of all things. Since no one listens, there can be no communication. The calls of the spiritually dying go unheard, and it is just as well, for were they answered only confusion and embarrassment would ensue.

Even so simple an activity as speaking on the telephone reflects the larger, moral implications of a society in which dialogue has all but ceased to exist; Norman is on the line with his brother; here is the way Irwin comes through to him: "I rannana rannana rannana all rannana rannana. *Rannana* rannana rannana! Rannana rannana rannana . . ." How else would his brother's harping speech sound to a man who sits "between daydream and nothing, looking at what was to be seen"? "Norman, are you listening?" asks Irwin, and the reply does nothing less than complete the quintessential exchange between monologist and monologist: " 'Of course,' he said without alarm. He knew that his lines didn't depend upon what his brother had been saying. 'The thing is, Irwin, in spite of all that . . .' " *(4)*. Although this negation allows Norman the time to interrupt his brother's monologue with one of his own—a litany of the breakdowns in the houses—his brother quickly regains the initiative and reduces him, if only temporarily, to simple sentences and monosyllables:

> "I'm not being unreasonable now, am I, Normy?"
> "Who ever said . . ."
> "It isn't too much for me to expect you to free me from these little things, is it?"
> "No, Irwin."

Fighting for a just cause, Norman will recover, and continuing his survey of what must be done at once to prevent disaster, he drives his brother to total exasperation, whereupon the latter promises money for the repairs and abruptly hangs up. For Norman, it is an empty victory.

As he makes his rounds, Moonbloom finds himself in nonrelation after nonrelation in which he answers the tenant's onslaught of rhetoric with cliché, palliative, or other perfunctory comment. Exuberant in his misery, sensitive only to obsession or complaint, the tenant, no more than the agent, wants, or is capable of, entering into a dialogue and an I-Thou relationship that would require a wholeness of personality he did not have and a commitment he could not make. In an extreme case—but all cases in the novel are extreme—Norman wonders whether the tenant "talked to himself when no one else was available. The words came out so fast and irrelevant to sensible response that only nodding and smiling were possible" (68). Thus the way of solipsism and the purer forms of monologue.

Here is a wholly typical exchange between Moonbloom and Sugarman, the railroad candy vendor:

> "How can you call yourself humorless, Sugarman? You're known as the wit of the rails."
> "I only cry out in the darkness as we rush through the countryside," Sugarman said. "My jokes are merely wails; my sounds of humor are cumulatively a dirge. Hey, don't I know—humor is tragic; it sinks the knife far deeper than solemnity. The laugh is as elemental as a baby's gas smile, a reflex of pain."
> "You're very eloquent, Sugarman," Norman said, as willing to kill time one way as another.... As far as he could tell, he derived the same pleasure, or sensation, from this as he did from the coin-induced foot vibrator he had used the week before. (58)

Sugarman demonstrates his eloquence in the very act of complaining that he is a failure, and Norman spends just as much emotion on him as he thinks he is worth. This is the very antithesis of communication and there will be no dialectical process to synthesize contradictions or produce meaning. Without communication, no unity, even though the tenants were all like "floaters in the lake of words to which they couldn't find a beginning or end" (96).

Furthermore, without communication, speech becomes purposeless, a thing-in-itself and a gratuity. Later explaining himself to Moonbloom in what passes for dialogue in an imperfect world, Sugarman says, " 'you are like a queer microphone into which my pent-up words can pour. To what purpose? God knows. Perhaps we all wish to be inscribed upon something. Maybe it has to do with perpetuating our silly little consciousnesses' " (139).

Now, it is through his monumental decision to do the repair work on all the apartments by himself that Moonbloom in effect enters the world, just as for the first time, as he tells us, " 'people entered me' " (209). One of the early examples of this experience occurs with Paxton, a black homosexual actor into whose life he has a momentary glimpse:

> "So I mess around with boys just to keep my prostate active, but in my work . . . I fuck the bejesus out of the world like

the biggest old bull this side of the labyrinth. And when I fly over that Atlantic Ocean, I really *do* fly. I goddamn well *soar!*"

And for once Moonbloom has the right reply: " 'It's amazing the funny ways people can fly. I have some hope of it myself.' " This elicits a compliment from Paxton (" 'Man, I think you'll make it, I truly do' "), and a "resonant moment" ensues in which the two sit in silence, appreciating "the deep courtesy that could occur between people" (209).

Thus, Moonbloom learns that language is not always an instrument of alienation, argument, insult, and complaint, but sometimes the means to intimacy, an insight that is confirmed and elaborated during his attempt to make the repairs:

> As a laborer in the tenants' kitchens and bathrooms, he assumed a familiarity that transformed his very species to them; people will tell their maids things they might hide from their immediate family. Underfoot, silent, diligent as a dog burying his bone, he seemed eminently trustworthy, as ideal for confidences as a religious image. To some, speaking nakedly in his presence was like talking to themselves.... One parades nakedness to provoke, but also it is an act of complete trust. Maybe he was an ear of God. (197–98)

This episode foreshadows the "dialogic event"—if it can be so called—that takes place when Norman is completing his last project, the repair of a wall bursting with sewage, aided by the super (Gaylord), the tenant (Basellecci), and a plumber (Bodien):

> They spoke constantly, yet none of them would remember afterward what they said. Heat and joy were generated; untold numbers of stories and reminiscences passed between them in an intimacy no normal men ever achieve. Norman's

head rang with the tremendous noise of the experience, his heart filled to bursting, burst, and went on. (242)

All the elements of a dialogical event are present here except the seriousness that is inherent in Buber's conception. We believe we should rejoice with Norman when he tells us,

> If we all reach our last day of life at the very same time, it will be something like this. He stole glances at the heathen faces of Bodien and Gaylord, the suffering, yet oddly consoled, eyes and mouth of Basellecci, noting the brave enthusiasm of men who had never dreamed of anything very definite, and it occurred to him . . . that there *was* only one hope for him, and for all people who had lost, through intelligence, the hope of immortality. "We must love and delight in each other and in ourselves!" he cried. (242–43)

All this is too sentimental for Norman, who ascribes it to drunkenness and tries to reduce it to absurdity:

> Sentiment had to disintegrate under what his drunken mind knew now, and in its place came an immense capacity to consume. He felt carnivorous, as though he could devour all of them, himself included. . . . Why, he was huge, united with all of them! His eyes, his brain, his ears, all swallowed the universe. "Oh my," he belched. (244)

But this passage is followed by what is apparently a transcendent moment of relation:

> Then, suddenly, a rosy glow suffused the new white plaster, and they were done and it was morning. Basellecci stood with a beatific expression on his wasted face, and the other three admired with him the straight gleaming wall.
> "It is done," Basellecci said with a serene smile. "What more could I have asked?"

In the final scene Norman meditates on the liberation of

his name and it would seem that he has experienced an aesthetic moment if not an epiphany.

There is no denying that Moonbloom and Friedman's Stern are very similar characters, facing similar problems of distance and relation. Stern's long-awaited showdown with the kike man, though not wholly satisfactory, opens the way to a silent but highly communicative moment with his wife and son; Moonbloom's completion of his labors, as we've just seen, leads to a virtually unspoken but intense moment of intimacy with those who have helped him and finally to a sense of his own freedom, although what this involves beyond a brief elation we do not fully know.

Moonbloom and Stern are also different, in at least one critical way. The source of anti-Semitism in Friedman's novel is the kike man, over whom Stern is obsessed; that in Wallant's work is a former Nazi, Ilse Moeller, a tenant who constantly baits Moonbloom in an effort to evoke his hatred. (The anti-Semitism of Wade Johnson, another tenant, seems to be more a matter of rhetoric than a deep-seated psychosis and therefore elicits no such response as that of Ilse.) For instance:

> "You seem to be not in a good mood, Moonbloom. Do I rub you in the wrong manner?"
> "I don't get your joke," he said harshly. . . .
> "Ah," she thought. " . . . he *is* human, he does feel something oppressive in me. . . ."
> "See, now it comes out," she said gaily. . . .
> "You do dislike me after all." (132–33)

Stern's obsession is but a dimension of his sensitivity to his Jewishness. Although he is not an observant Jew, although he yearns to be accepted by gentile society, everything he says and does is motivated by his sense that he *is* Jewish. But this is not Moonbloom's problem. Quite the contrary, the question of being a Jew scarcely enters into his thoughts. Thus, even though he might "look" Jewish, and betray Jewish mannerisms in speech and gesture, he is actually suffering from the psychological and spiritual malaises of the Existential Man. Uncommitted to person, place, or thing, he protects himself from a demanding and invasive world every time he takes out his receipt book and thereby signals his imminent departure.

Far from indicating that underneath it all Moonbloom is a Jew, Ilse Moeller's success in provoking him does nothing more than demonstrate how much it takes to arouse anyone so fundamentally apathetic. Nor does it really matter that most of Moonbloom's tenants have Jewish names; most of them are not especially Jewish in manner or in the problems they suffer and they seem to be no different in kind or degree from their *goyische* neighbors. If certain characters are meant to be taken as being Jewish for good reason, they are presented *pares cum paribus* and are not particularly central to the themes or structure of the novel.

If being a Jew is not thematically important to *The Tenants of Moonbloom,* it is critical to the meaning of Wallant's *The Pawnbroker* and its pathologically alienated hero, Sol Nazerman. *Tenants* is a comic novel, *The Pawnbroker* a tragic one. Although monologue is everywhere apparent in the former, some kind of dialogue is still possible, and this is so because boredom or ennui are the chief sources of despair and such despair can be alleviated by distraction and eliminated by relation. We recall that in the existential situation anxiety (*angoisse*) is general and undetermined, a metaphysical and psychological given; Roquentin is intended to speak for modern man, and in a sense so is Moonbloom. But Nazerman is not: his whole character, everything that he suffers, is a direct consequence of his being Jewish and a victim of the Holocaust, in which his family was literally destroyed and he himself transformed into a living dead man. If some form of dialogue is possible in Moonbloom's world, it is inconceivable in Nazerman's. Every utterance he makes, even during charitable acts, stems from *refusal—*

2. The Monological Jew in Fiction

refusal of sympathy, of intimacy, of love, of, indeed, the very idea of relation. It is not, I repeat, the refusal of the existential or absurdist hero, which, after its negations, leaves open the question of affirmation. Rather it is the ultimate Refusal, of humanity no less than of God, and its nihilism makes that of Sartre and Camus seem paltry in comparison.

Antihumanism means antidialogue, antilanguage, antirelation. Wallant has a particular talent for dramatizing this abstraction, so vital to the meaning of the whole novel. Here is an exchange between Nazerman and Marilyn Birchfield, a woman seeking to befriend him:

> "Will you come to dinner, Sol?"
> "No-thank-you," he said, like someone who knew just those three words of a foreign language. . . .
> "Oh, you're busy then. Well, perhaps later in the week, maybe Friday. How would that suit you?"
> "There is no point to it."
> "I don't understand."
> "You don't understand," he echoed. "Let me be clearer then. There is no point to any relationship between us, *no point at all.* . . ."
> "I believe there *could* be a point to our relationship, at least for me. I like you and I enjoy being with you and talking with you. . . ."
> "Do not think of becoming intimate with me. For your own good I say this. . . . You would be guilty of necrophilia. It is obscene to love the dead." (161–62)

Nazerman's voice is that of the Holocaust, forever beyond the range of hearing of the "normal" human being. Marilyn Birchfield, social worker, decent, rational, liberal, caring, has no idea that she is responding to a fourth-dimensional phenomenon in three-dimensional terms, that her attempt to understand and help Nazerman is as naïve and futile as that of reason trying to master the Absurd, of normal instincts trying to deal with utter horror, or simply as that of the living seeking to converse with the dead. On what basis can the *o*'s escape from Nazerman's name—that name so suggestively close to that of the very evil itself that has all but destroyed its bearer? It is not, certainly, that Nazerman is a Nazi in any common definition of the term; he is a "nazi" because in his extreme victimization he is "non-human," unapproachable, beyond discourse.[1] He inhabits a world in which all humanistic values, motives, and feelings are suspended, and, dialogue being impossible, all relations are radically I-It.

In the denouement Jésus Ortiz, Nazerman's assistant, conspires with two of his friends to rob the pawnshop. When one of the gang threatens to shoot Nazerman, Ortiz, who never intended any harm to Nazerman, tries to shield him and is shot.

The novel concludes with Nazerman overcome with weeping. I find it difficult to believe that this release points toward salvation or the emergence of a Nazerman reborn into the human race. Such a conclusion would undermine the whole vision of the Holocaust as a totally dehumanizing and dehumanized event, from which there were no survivors. And isn't that Wallant's real theme—that Nazerman cannot free himself from the agony of memory any more than he can eradicate the numbers tattooed on his arm, that having in effect died at Auschwitz, he will not be resurrected in Harlem, for there is no Messiah and Jesus does not save even when he is shot trying?[2]

5 Carnivalizing the Logos

In his more than two dozen works, the best known of which are *The Education of Hyman Kaplan* and *The Joys of Yiddish,* Leo Rosten has established himself as a voice of Jewish humor and a spokesman of the middle-class values that are reflected in it. If we can believe the dust-jacket testimonials of *Silky!*—"a Yiddish version of *The Maltese Falcon*" as one newspaper has it—Rosten is one of "America's most talented and versatile writers" and *Silky!* a brilliant comic success. Said to be "one of a kind—funny, resourceful, glib and gutsy," by one reviewer, Silky is proclaimed by another to be a charmer, his narration a treat, and the glossary that he has concocted himself a delight.

If all this enthusiasm is not a hoax (one can never be sure with Rosten), I must say that I find it misplaced. Rosten is simply not *that* funny nor is Silky *that* amusing; the humor rarely rises above the Borsch Circuit–nightclub variety that elicits a response from those who would laugh out loud at anything slightly off-color. But *Silky!* is interesting for that very reason and the Hyman Kaplan books no less so.

Rosten wants us to accept Silky as a pop-art hero, and while he may in some ways be a parody of Sam Spade, the hard-boiled, womanizing sleuth that Bogart helped make into an American folk-hero, Silky must finally be judged as a character in his own right. "With *chutzpah* as big as the Bronx and an armory of wit," says another testimonial, he "has to be some sort of genius. He will surely enter the gallery of great private eyes." (And, I suspect, come flying out the back door!)

Aside from his facility with language, which we'll be looking at more closely in a moment, his Jewishness also poses a question involving his character and its moral significance. And so, finally, does his sexism, which, although a convention of the hard-boiled private eye genre, is too much a part of Silky's personality to be dismissed as mere parody.

To begin with, what poses a problem for us about Silky's being a Jew is that it poses no problem for him. In all his relations with the underworld, the few anti-Semitic incidents that he endures never get beyond the talking stage or develop into a serious threat. Thus, while the streets might be a jungle, they are not especially dangerous for Jews. In a situation in which a Jew has an Irish Catholic for a partner—and one with a weakness for the joys of Yiddish at that—then, whatever the other threats, all is possible to him.

It is true that he is the member of a violent profession and therefore would be held contemptible by the Scriptures. What saves him on this score is precisely the fact that he is a wordsman and not, at heart, a gunman, and to be a good wordsman is, in the myth, to be a Jew. The real question is, what kind of a wordsman is he?

As a man who gets by with shrewdness and wit against opponents who speak his language and whose language he speaks (street American, a smattering of Yiddish, mostly abrasive, and, when required, standard English), as a man fully in control of himself and usually of others, both enemies and female clients, Silky is no stereotype of the *shlemiel* by which the low comic Jew is most often characterized. But neither is he depicted in the truly human dimensions of the Jew as he actually is.[1]

Far from being a figure who could enter into a dialogue,

2. The Monological Jew in Fiction

and therefore into a genuinely intimate relation with others, he is revealed as a kind of *anti-shlemiel*, a fantasized hero, but one who would be cheered on mainly by the audience in a vaudeville house. Here, then, is Silky's description of the entrance of Kimberley Marsh (an analogue rather than a parody of "Miss Wonderly's" into Spade's office):

> She didn't walk in, you have to understand; she floated in, cool and clean and so beautiful it hurt.... a whiff of perfume out of Baghdad. And when I get a load of her architecture.... She is—she is ravishing.... Hair the color of honey and smooth with sheen. A skin, peaches and cream. A mouth, a red tulip.... And stacked?! ... wham! went my heart.
> Do I sound like a pushover? [he adds] Listen. I have knocked over more than my quota of quiff, some of them fantastic, but never ... did anyone hit me like this. (4)

This is the kind of emotional response to a woman permitted the hard-boiled private detective, just as the crass clichés that express it are offered as high amusement. Since this response is consistently maintained throughout the novel, until its ecstatic consummation, we have no reason to doubt its sincerity—not that it really matters. Silky is smitten not by love but with lust, and his idiom demonstrates his inability to see Kimberley as anything but an object and to describe her in any but sexist terms. His relationships in general never transcend the "I-It"; therefore, he never engages in authentic dialogue but speaks a language designed to intimidate, impress, or manipulate an adversary, a category to which all others, friend, foe, or lover, are sooner or later relegated.

Ironically, in his need to dominate every conversation in which he engages, the predatory monologist is himself pursued by the Furies of Language, who demand witticism and wise-talk every time he opens his mouth. Silky is not so astute as he thinks he is—nor as Rosten does—in placating them, as this conversation makes painfully obvious. Accused by Kimberley of ogling her, Silky replies:

> "Maybe I'm looking at you 'that way' because you've been putting me through a ringer looking at *me* 'that way.' What are you, aside from flaky—a nympho?"
> ... "Temper ... *Tem*-per."
> "You leave your blouse open practicly [sic] down to your pupik—that means navel, Miss Marsh—and you swish your hips and cross your legs like you're auditioning for the Dietrich part in *Blue Angel*. Is this how you charge your batteries? Giving the boys hot nuts?"
> "Don't be vulgar!"
> "Vulgar-shmulgar, knock it off. You're the sexpot, not me...
> "Oh, my," she slow grins. "Aren't you the jealous one?!"
> "Plenty. The gut point is: Do you want protection or do you want to get laid?" (19-20)

Under this verbal onslaught, with its supposedly no-nonsense logic, its aggressive Yiddishisms, its slangy and profane overstatement, is it any wonder that "Miss Marsh" is reduced to the banal and witless replies by which she seeks to defend herself? Of course, Silky succeeds in getting her to break a date and have dinner with him, therefore confirming that women are invariably attracted to men who abuse them and that inarticulate but beautiful blonde *shikses* find loud-mouthed curly-haired Jewish private detectives irresistible—just so long as they aren't *shlemiels*.

Can we doubt that Silky will talk his way into bed with his lady? We don't and he does. Here is his description of the great moment that, through double-entendre, innuendo, pun, and plain crudity, he has been seeking from the beginning of the novel:

> I suppose I should describe the moans she moaned, the way her hot body moved into me and trembled when I touched the little man in the rowboat, and her burning

mouth as I opened my mouth and surrounded her lips and sucked in her sweet, sweet tongue, and her cries of "Oh! Oh! Lover! Yes, yes, yes!" and her flaming, pulsing wetness as I slid into her, faster and harder. . . . And when she came, she screamed and it was like a hundred Baked Alaskas exploded for us and lit up the blue dark of the room. (191)

I don't begrudge the hero his exploding Baked Alaskas—in fact, for a moment I feared that Rosten intended to deprive him of this ultimate treat, thereby demonstrating that, as we suspected, Silky was all talk. But no, the happy day arrives when he takes his clothes off "faster than any fireman ever put his on" and dives into the sack with his *tsatske*. His account is completely in character: the event is entirely physical, sensation replaces feeling, and it all ends in a shriek. Thus Kimberley, wholly the proverbial sex-object, is brought to the heights of affirmation without the soliloquy of a Molly Bloom to save her from the pornography that is her lover's natural mode of expression. No matter how ecstatic, mere copulation is not sexual love, for it engenders no true intimacy or language, no sense of one's wholeness or awareness not only of the body of the partner, but of his or her "presence."

Convention dictates that the private eye gets the girl but doesn't have to, or shouldn't, marry her. And Jewish tradition places a taboo on intermarriage. So Silky is doubly protected against becoming domesticated, even if he had it in him to propose in the first place. By the logic of things Kimberley must be done away with, and she dies following a shootout from which Silky emerges a hero in no danger of tarnishing his image. Still, we can't be sure he had an image to be tarnished in the first place. For all his domineering presence, he is spiritually an absence; and all his palaver can't make him anything more than the monological man he is.

Although there is no certainty that *The Education of Hyman*

Kaplan (that is to say, *T*h*e E*d*u*c*a*t*i*o*n o*f H*y*m*a*n K*a*p*l*a*n*) and its sequels are any more allegorical than *Silky!*, certain themes may be heard, if one listens carefully, beyond the din of pregnant mispronunciations, malapropisms, puns, and other derangements of language produced in the beginner's class of the American Night Preparatory School for Adults.[2] What speakers of Yiddish can do to the English language is a source of never ending delight to Rosten and this phenomenon seems to be the *raison d'être* of the novel; despite the title, neither Hyman Kaplan nor his teacher, Mr. Parkhill, undergoes any real development or experiences any rite of passage.

Although the class contains members of over a half dozen ethnic groups, not even a hint of prejudice exists; and none of these characters has much of an existence beyond his classroom performance and the stereotyped anxieties that motivate him. An antagonism between Kaplan— aggressive, eccentric, stubborn—and several of the students who can't abide him provides much of the drama, but, again, it is too inconsistent to create much suspense or yield any meaning.

If meaning does exist in the work, the key to it is, I believe, in Parkhill's relation (or nonrelation) to Hyman Kaplan, whose liberties with English, no less than his character in general, seem to spring from hidden and mysterious causes that Parkhill is virtually obsessed with discovering. Despite this obsession, Parkhill is not intended to be taken as a neurotic or, in contrast to the usual low comic stereotype of the teacher, a pedant. On the contrary, Rosten informs us that Parkhill is a man of "patience," "kindliness, and fortitude": "He never loses faith in the possibility of teaching anyone the rudiments of English" (x). *Rudiments*: herein lies a clue to the whole problem, for Parkhill is, as no doubt his syllabus requires, devoted to rudiments to the exclusion of everything else.

There isn't a page in the book that doesn't show Parkhill mediating a dispute over definition or a point of grammar,

2. The Monological Jew in Fiction

correcting the errors of an oral report or a theme transcribed on the blackboard; outside class, we find him no less diligently grading papers and thinking up new ways of eliciting standard English from his pupils. All this is laudable and no doubt necessary. The trouble is that anything that threatens to overflow the narrow banks of English grammar and vocabulary is quickly rechanneled or dried up by neglect. Student autobiographies are read only for use of language, even when—especially when—beneath their inarticulateness they reveal suffering or powerful emotions. When Kaplan submits an essay on his job complaining about working conditions ("Why should we svet and slafe in a dark place by chip laktric and all kinds hot? For who? A Boss who is salfish, fat, driving a fency automobil??"), Parkhill tells him, "We must confine ourselves to simple exercises . . . before we attempt political essays." And Kaplan replies, "So naxt time should be no *ideas*. . . . Only plain fects?" " 'F*a*cts, Mr. Kaplan, not f*e*cts,' " answers Parkhill (26).

That one stick to the facts of grammar and vocabulary, attend conscientiously to one's accent, and in general exercise self-restraint are, as I have implied, principles essential to a successful language class. But the matter doesn't end here. I have said that Parkhill is no tyrant—not consciously, anyway. But he is the Authority, keeper of the arcana of the English language, and therefore to be held in awe. Securely founded on grammar, however, this authority extends to other less innocuous areas, for Parkhill is also a part of a system, the aim of which is to turn foreigners into Americans. Speaking correct English is necessary to being an American, and each correction of one's words is just that much more foreign dross melted away. Since the goal is cultural conformity, one's concentration on grammar is itself a political act. Parkhill may not be a tyrant but he is a zealot, and, as far as engaging his class in dialogue (and all that it means) is concerned, it is the same thing. "Just as grandfather brought God to the heathen, I bring Grammar to the alien," he tells his aunt, who thinks that night school is *infra dig*. The association of conversion with assimilation would be the final step in an American solution to the non-Christian immigrant problem—that means Jews, chiefly—but nothing, I daresay, could be farther from Parkhill's mind. He is too busy worrying about how to explain gerunds to the class and equally important how to control Kaplan and make sense of his behavior.

In a way Parkhill is the defender of what Ferdinand de Saussure has called *la langue,* language in its formal, systematic, standard aspect, as embodied in principles and rules, in contradistinction to *la parole,* language as it is actually spoken in all its idiomatic and colloquial irregularity. Even more relevantly, Parkhill is "monological," not only in Buber's sense, which we'll deal with shortly, but also in that of M. M. Bakhtin, the Russian formalist who is currently undergoing a revival for his studies of narrative discourse.

As in Buber, the central conception in Bakhtin lies in the distinction between monologue and dialogue, although Bakhtin, not a theologian, is interested in a somewhat different issue. He sees monologue, for instance, as a fixed utterance, a closed statement made to a passive listener. Self-sufficient and hermetic, it does not enter into *relation* with other utterances (just as in Buber the monologist does not enter into relation with others). Expressing the unitary and the centric, it speaks with and for authority and the established order.

Dialogue, on the other hand, expresses the *heteroglossia* (the polyglot nature) of a given society. Here, unlike monologue, which is "mono-semic," "there is a constant interaction between meanings, all of which have the potential of conditioning the others." Whereas monologue is fixed and complete, dialogue is open-ended, dynamic, changing, and "centrifugal" (a "decentering force").

These distinctions apply mainly to the novel, where there may be a single authorial voice that dominates and orchestrates all of the many voices in the world it depicts (Tolstoy),

2. The Monological Jew in Fiction

or there may be many voices in an unorchestrated polyglot in which no hierarchy is possible and all voices have equal value (Dostoevsky). This conception also applies to the night school, where the monological instructor faces the polyphonic class.

As their voluntary attendance and awe of Parkhill would indicate, the dialogical students consciously desire to be "orchestrated" or assimilated. On the other hand, in low comic style, they have a natural tendency to reduce everything to absurdity. We might read this disruption as the triumph of immigrant anarchy over Anglo-Saxon order or even as that of *parole* over *langue* or proletarian over bourgeois. Bakhtin might see in it the process of "carnivalization," by which the low and comic subvert authority and herald a revitalized social order.

As described by Bakhtin in *Rabelais and His World*, carnivalization was a medieval folkway in which, during festive occasions, social hierarchies—"privileges, norms, prohibitions"—were temporarily suspended and a rough egalitarianism prevailed. "Carnival was the true feast of time," says Bakhtin, "the feast of becoming, change, and renewal" (10). Essentially a collective act, it stood for wholeness and the vital interaction of things as opposed to the individualistic, isolated, and static world perceived by the Renaissance. Bakhtin's distinctions are in accord with the basic Marxist view of reality, although "grotesque realism," Bakhtin's term for this view, might not in all its aspects be to Marx's liking, nor, probably, would Bakhtin's neglect of the economic distinctions between classes that existed in the historical periods under discussion.

All the disruptive elements of carnival are present in the Columbus Day episode, which ends in a shambles of pedagogy and patriotism, two expressions of established society. Parkhill has little idea, in his announcement, that he is courting disaster: "Tonight, class, let us set aside our routine tasks for a while to discuss the man whose historic achievement our country will commemorate tomorrow." A

Carnivalizing the Logos 63

momentous statement in appropriately formal diction—Parkhill is announcing the temporary suspension of the exclusive concern for grammatical detail that rules the class. (It is a dangerous decision but an inevitable one arising from the contradictions of the system. The ceremony is designed to inspire patriotism and therefore advance the process of assimilation, but at the same time it opens a pandora's box that the exclusive study of grammar kept closed.) Parkhill continues, "To this man ... America owes its very beginning. I'm sure you all know whom I mean—" Then the farce begins:

> "Jawdgie Washington!" Isaac Nussbaum promptly guessed.
> "No, not 'Georgie'—*George*—Washington. I was referring to another—" [Parkhill can't refrain from correcting Nussbaum's pronunciation of George. I don't think that Nussbaum is profaning the great man by using the diminutive—just following an "Americanization" of the Russian "Georgy".]
> "Cortez?" asked Lola Lopez. "Ricardo Cortez?"
> "That's a moom-picture actor!" Nathan P. Nathan could hardly contain his laughter. . . .
> "Paul Rewere!" cried Oscar Trabish. . . .
> "Not Paul 'Rewere,'" sighed Mr. Parkhill [etc.].

When he asks, "What *date* is tomorrow?," Parkhill gets this reply:

> "Dat's mine *boitday*! October tvalf! I should live so!"
> It was (but why, oh why, did it have to be?) Hyman Kaplan. (206–7)

And we're off on the subject of Kaplan's birthday.

This *reductio* of the Columbus Day exercise ends in a verbal brawl created by Kaplan's opinions on such subjects as the worthiness of Admiral Byrd (Edmiral Boyd) to be compared to "Columbiss" and the failure of Ferdinand and

2. The Monological Jew in Fiction

Isabella to supply Columbus with "batter transportation." Kaplan thus whips up a storm of outrage from trivia, irrelevancy, and nonsequitur: "And now the battle soared— with shouts and cries and accusations; with righteous assaults on the Kaplan logic, and impassioned defenses...."

Kaplan is the one member of the class able to disconcert Parkhill, who sees him as an anomaly in all he says and does. Characteristically, he resolves to treat Kaplan, despite his "distressing diction, his wayward grammar, his outlandish spelling," the same way he treated every other student (79). He makes this resolution precisely because he believes that, far from being like every other pupil, Kaplan is *sui generis*, "some sort of cosmic force, a reckless, independent star that swam through the heavens in its own unpredictable orbit" (230–31). But insofar as he is *sui generis* he is the Unassimilatable Man, who menaces the entire program. None of these keys to Kaplan's character, however, really satisfies Parkhill, and he continues to generate solutions that prove only the durability of his anxiety. Thus Parkhill never does win his battle to gain the ultimate insight into Kaplan's mind or to reduce him to another student-in-the-class and thereby eliminate the threat to the English language that he represents.

Now, Parkhill is a monologist in Buber's sense of the word as well as Bakhtin's. In *Between Man and Man* Buber writes that

> the will to educate ... may degenerate into arbitrariness, and.... the educator may carry out his selection and his influence from himself and his idea of the pupil, not from the pupil's own reality.... [He] must at the same time be over there, on the surface of that other spirit [pupil] ... of this individual and unique being which is being acted upon—not of some conceptual, contrived spirit, but all the time the wholly concrete spirit of this individual and unique being who is living and confronting him.... It is not enough for him to imagine the [pupil's] individuality.... Only when he ... feels how it affects one ... does he rec-

ognize the real limit, baptize his self-will in Reality and make it true will...." (100)

I am aware that this abstract and dense view hardly seems appropriate to Rosten's comic work and its one- or two-dimensional characters. Yet there is a lesson here and it's worth speculating upon. Buber is talking about the "dialogical event" as it is to occur in the classroom. Elsewhere he argues against the lecture as a pedagogical method and for the kind of dialogue in which the "whole being" of the teacher affects the whole being of the pupil: "you ... need a man who is wholly alive and able to communicate himself directly to his fellow beings.... [He] affects them most strongly and purely when he has no thought of affecting them" (105).

It is true that Buber is here talking about humanistic education, not language training. Parkhill is not being paid to enter into I-Thou dialogue with his students; on the other hand, he has a sense of mission. And it is precisely this sense that causes him to yearn to be an educator while making it impossible for him to be one.

We have already seen that for Parkhill language instruction is but a stepping stone to full assimilation, the school being "an incubator of Citizens." His own calling has been "to imbue men and women from a dozen nations with the meaning of America—its dramatic past, its precious traditions, its noblest aspirations."

Parkhill is so immersed in his vocation, it would be impossible for him to identify himself with any alien reality or, indeed, have any understanding of its nature. His relation with his students can never reach the level of I-Thou communication because they are for him merely the raw material that he must refine, objects to be molded to design and put into the American mainstream. Hopelessly trapped in an I-It situation (and the more certain he is of his grammar, the fewer chances he has of reaching Kaplan and the class), he is committed to imposing grammatical rules and laws upon his polyglot pupils who, intimidated by his knowledge, accept all he tells them.

Language, which should open a way to communication between teacher and class, is actually a barrier to empathy and understanding. Because he speaks nothing but American English there is no way Parkhill can communicate with his students on any but the most primitive levels. And they in their turn speak nothing but an inchoate English that Parkhill will listen to, never for ideas and feelings, but only for pronunciation and correct usage.

Thus Kaplan appears to Parkhill not in his full person but only through an indecorous Yiddish-English—a Yiddish carnivalization of English that hints of idiosyncrasy, gratuity, and disruption. What, then, is Kaplan's "full person"? (By this term I mean the "whole self" that participates in true I-Thou dialogue.) To begin with, I have mentioned that no anti-Semitism exists in the "polyphonic" class and also that, despite the accents, expressions, and names, Jewishness as such is never an important factor in the interrelations of the students. In any event Parkhill, thoroughly the American, has no real inkling of what Jewishness is or what Jews are.

Until he does, he can never penetrate the mystery that he associates with Kaplan, who is Jewish to the core and so accepting of himself that he has lost all self-consciousness about it. Far from seeing himself as the challenge to authority and the menace that Parkhill takes him to be, Kaplan thinks that he is furthering the progress of the class every time he opens his mouth; he has no more idea of the impression he is making on Parkhill than Parkhill has of what and who Kaplan is.

The day could come when Parkhill loses his innocence and learns the human reality behind his carnival student, apprehends Kaplan in his wholeness (Jewishness)—a totality greater than the sum of its attributes. Then Kaplan, the noncommunicating monologist, who seems to be a law unto himself, might awaken to his full person. On that day both would learn the meaning of anti-Semitism but they might also find the way to dialogue. The carnival spirit degrades to uplift, destroys to resurrect, finds rebirth in all death—so there might be reason for hope. But carnival being medieval and cynicism being modern, we cannot help wondering what language will be used in the dialogue and what the two will have to say to each other.

6 The New Jersey Jews and Their Pagan Gods

In one of the more curious episodes of Philip Roth's *Goodbye, Columbus*, the hero, Neil Klugman, awaiting in St. Patrick's Cathedral the return of his lover, Brenda Patimkin, from her efforts to obtain the diaphragm he has insisted upon, attempts to engage God in a dialogue. We need not ask the obvious question, What is a good Jewish boy trying to find in a cathedral in the first place? Neil, while no Christian, is no good Jewish boy, either, though Brenda, whose family is nouveau riche, will, it turns out, be a good "Jewish princess." Actually, Neil has gone into the cathedral to escape the heat and it is with much self-consciousness that he finds himself, though refusing to kneel, uttering a prayer:

> God ... I am twenty-three years old. I want to make the best of things. Now the doctor is about to wed Brenda to me, and I am not entirely certain this is all for the best. What is it I love, Lord? Why have I chosen? Who is Brenda? The race is to the swift. Should I have stopped to think?
>
> I was getting no answers, but I went on. If we meet you at all, God, it's that we're carnal, and acquisitive, and thereby partake of You. I am carnal, and I know You approve, I just know it. But how carnal can I get? I am acquisitive. Where do I turn now in my acquisitiveness? Where do we meet? Which prize is You?

It was an ingenious meditation, and suddenly I felt ashamed. I got up and walked outside, and the noise of Fifth Avenue met me with an answer:

Which prize do you think, *shmuck?* Gold dinnerware, sporting-goods trees, nectarines, garbage disposals, bumpless noses, Patimkin Sink, Bonwit Teller—

But damn it, God, that *is* You!

And God only laughed, that clown. (100)

"It was an ingenious meditation": in this self-conscious and not quite self-congratulatory assessment by Neil lies, I'd say, the key to what is wrong with the prayer and with Neil's whole life. Ill at ease among the Patimkins, those *Alrightniks* who have risen above the hot plains of Newark to air-conditioned Short Hills, he is no more at home with his overpowering Aunt Gladys, who *shtups* him with enough food to feed an army and more than enough advice to drive him *meshugge*. At once condescending to and intimidated by both families, who represent the economic and social poles of the Jewish population, Neil has no context, authority, or source to confirm his judgments or to establish a social identity. Thus he can engage in no genuine dialogue with any of the primary characters, most of whom are, themselves, incapable of carrying on a true conversation. Aunt Gladys, for instance, speaks according to a logic of verbal aggression that renders all reply meaningless and often forces Neil to defend himself against an onslaught of cooking and comments at the same time:

I forked a potato in half and ate it, while Aunt Gladys, who had seated herself across from me, watched. "You don't want bread," she said, "I wouldn't cut it it should go stale."

"I *want* bread," I said.

"You don't like with seeds, do you?" I tore a piece of bread in half and ate it.

"How's the meat?" she said.

"Okay, good."

"You'll fill yourself with potatoes and bread, the meat you'll leave over I'll have to throw it out."

2. The Monological Jew in Fiction

(This last statement is not a true run-on sentence. The parts are so closely linked in logic and spirit it would be sacrilegious to separate them with any punctuation stronger than a comma, and sometimes even that's too much.)

Aunt Gladys is only one avatar of the domineering Jewish mother for whom "hocking" with words is an analogue to "shtupping" with food, each of these acts becoming most effective when combined and the victim suffers not only the food itself but also the monologue, the incessant instruction, opinion, and observation, that accompanies its serving.[1] Among the more formidable literary incarnations of the "Yiddische Mama," Sophie Portnoy (*Portnoy's Complaint*), Meg (Friedman's *A Mother's Kisses*), Frieda Gold (Herbert Gold's *Family*), and Bessie Berger (Clifford Odets' *Awake and Sing!*) are all treated as comic characters who wield a power that, being a source of family unity and family disintegration, is anything but comic.[2] In one sense the urge-to-feed is a part of motherhood, no more, no less; carried to an extreme, it reverses itself and turns its devotees into cannibals whose deities are strictly pagan. "Oy, he's such a fine boy I could eat him up"—so goes a line in a Yiddish joke and it is not just a manner of speaking.

Although rarely resulting in physical assault, the violence that marks the colorful diction of these women when they are being sarcastic or abusive can go beyond mere words and into gesture, as when Sophie Portnoy holds a knife to her son to insure that he will clean his plate. We need not go into the psychology or the politics of this phenomenon; it is enough to say that if these women kill their children with kindness, they also devour them in the act of nourishing them. (Portnoy's "complaint" is, no doubt, one form of response to a mother who seems capable of carrying out the ultimate Freudian threat.)[3] They also "consume" the father, who, often a failure in business or otherwise penurious, hangs around the house in pale imitation of his forebears who studied the Talmud all day while the women did all the labor.

Explaining "gastrolatry," worship of the stomach god, Bakhtin points out the saving nature of this kind of devotion. The god, Gaster, is the "inventor and creator of all mankind's technology." Gluttony is but the result of abundant food (*Rabelais and His World*, 304). Following this logic, we can, perhaps, be more charitable in our judgment of the Jewish mother. In his study of Odets' use of Yinglish (Yiddish-English) in *Awake and Sing!*, for example, Harold Cantor sees a context of Jewish tradition and heritage that lends meaning to both the speech and preoccupation with food that characterizes Bessie Berg. Extolling Odets' mastery of the "psychology of dialect as dialogue," Cantor cites Bessie's way of asking Jacob whether he's fed the dog ("You gave the dog eat?"), along with Jacob's reply ("I gave the dog eat"). Cantor sees in this "an entire complex of understandings," one that involves recollection by the Jews in the audience of the "biblical and talmudic injunctions for the care and nourishment of cattle and sheep, which is an ancestral memory of a formerly nomadic people" (64). He also detects a ritualistic quality in the question and answer to which anyone accustomed to incantation would respond. But, Cantor notes, Jews in the shtetls never kept dogs or cats as pets and that Bessie's concern for "Tootsie" is part of her acculturation to American values, a source of pride "evinced moments later when she defends her pet to Schlosser, the janitor: 'Tootsie's making dirty in the hall? . . . Tootsie walks behind me like a lady, any time, any place.'"

I am aware that Cantor is trying to demonstrate Odets' ability to create a language for his characters that would appeal to both gentiles and Jews in the audience. Still, his argument involves a characterization of Bessie that is speculative if not farfetched. Is Bessie's concern for Tootsie's dinner evidence of her Americanization or simply another facet of her urge to feed every one and every thing—man, woman, child, and animal—that falls under her hegemony? Is it pride that makes her reply to Schlosser as she does or insensitivity to the feelings or rights of anyone or anything that falls beyond—namely, the *goyim*?

Conceding the Jewish tendency to "identify verbally intense anguish and emotion with the digestive process," Cantor hears in Bessie's disgusted "In a minute I'll get up from the table. I can't take a bite in my mouth no more" echoes of a Jewish past of "frequent famine and starvation." And he goes on to suggest that the collective recollection of past hunger is one reason the Bergers "are constantly *eating* in this play." I submit that Bessie's announcement is tied not so much to a past hunger as a present one equally great and much more immediate; when she says she is so disgusted she cannot eat, she means she is *disgusted*. If the Bergers are constantly eating, it has little to do, I think, with actual hunger, past or present; they eat because Bessie sees to it that they do. And she sees to it because when they eat so (in a manner of speaking) does she, and her "appetite" is as insatiable as her need for domestic power.

Cantor indicates what is up to a point a central fact about Bessie's world—that it is in essence monological. As Robert Warshow put it, according to Cantor, "it is as if no one really listens to anyone else; each takes his own line, and the significant connections between one speech and another are not in logic but in the heavy emotional climate of the family." I'm not sure I understand exactly what is meant here by "heavy emotional climate," with its implication that the Bergers, at some point in their relationships, engage each other in dialogue and reach a state of authentic, if "illogical," communication. I do understand that it is Cantor's purpose in his essay to locate this kind of communication in the social psychology of Yiddish, but I believe he is, as I have implied, on shaky ground. There can be no dialogue between the members of the family until Bessie makes it possible by actually listening to others, and since power is in root and branch monological and converses only with itself, that is not going to happen.

Comparing Michael Gold's view of the Jewish mother to Roth's, Barry Gross argues that Gold sees her as a heroine because he is measuring her with Jewish standards, while Roth sees her as "domineering, nagging, neurotic, paranoid, ethnocentric, castrating" because he measures her according to American standards (Gross, 174). Alexander Portnoy, he thinks, is self-deluded if he believes that he is a victim of Sophie, who on careful inspection proves to stand for "duty, discipline, and obedience," the foundation of Jewish values. "Portnoy's complaint against his mother is, in effect, a complaint against his being Jewish." This is true; furthermore, in repudiating his family, Portnoy asserts the freedom-for-nothing that characterizes the independent life of the rebellious generation. He enters into the total narcissism that manifests itself most obviously in toilet activity and in the monologism in which he is allowed to indulge by his position on the psychiatrist's couch and as the putative narrator of the book in which he appears.

Heroine or tyrant, matriarch or cannibal, the Jewish mother is not blameless for desertion by her son. If Alexander doesn't exactly gain our admiration for the kind of happiness he pursues, he at least has our sympathy, and so does Neil Klugman in his flight from Aunt Gladys to where?—to the world ruled by Mother Patimkin. Out of the frying pan into the fire (as it were)!

A conversation with Brenda's mother gives us an insight into Neil's dubious ability to defend himself against a figure no less powerful than the Jewish Mother—namely the Jewish Mother Suburbanized. Significantly, the subject is his Judaism; his only line of defense, evasion:

> "We're all going to Temple Friday night. Why don't you come with us? I mean are you orthodox or conservative?"
> I considered. "Well, I haven't gone in a long time . . . I sort of switch. . . ." I smiled. "I'm just Jewish," I said well-

2. The Monological Jew in Fiction

> meaningly.... Desperately I tried to think of something that would convince her I wasn't an infidel. Finally I asked: "Do you know Martin Buber's work?"
> "Buber... Buber," she said.... "Is he orthodox or conservative?" she asked.
> "... He's a philosopher."
> "Is he reformed?" she asked....
> "Orthodox," I said faintly.
> "That's very nice," she said....
> "Isn't Hudson Street Synagogue orthodox?" [she added]
> "I don't know."
> "I thought you belonged."
> "I was bar mitzvahed there."
> "And you don't know that it's orthodox?"
> "Yes I do. It is."
> "Then you must be."
> "Oh, yes, I am...." (88)

Finally, after more of this business, the phone rings and Neil tells us that he "spoke a silent orthodox prayer to the Lord." This is much more a concluding witticism than a sign of piety; Neil is neither orthodox, conservative, nor reformed—all distinctions for a middle-class Judaism in which he takes no share and has been warding off in the guise of Aunt Gladys for a good part of his life.

Nor is his prayer in the cathedral—a prayer that in its flippancy plays to an audience—anything more than the kind of parody in which a person like Neil would take delight. Now, I do not think that Buber's ideas on genuine prayer will overly distract us from the basically comic intent of this passage, and Buber tells us in *Eclipse of God* that the fundamental presupposition of prayer is that "the divine Presence become dialogically perceivable"—the guiding principle here being that he "who is not present perceives no Presence."

That is, one must be ready for Presence, to be in a state of "simple turned-towardness, unreserved spontaneity."

One is not ready when, engaged in "subjective reflection," he suffers the "over-consciousness" that "he is praying, that he is *praying*, that *he* is praying." "Can I call the self-conscious words I spoke prayer?" asks Neil. And when he finishes, he comments to himself, as we have seen, "It was an ingenious meditation." Having no God, Neil must concoct one and the one he concocts—being a carnivalization of himself—can give him only tautology or silence. Neil certainly cannot find an answer to his overwhelming question (Should I marry Brenda?) by carrying on a monologue with an imagined audience called God Who inevitably turns out to be a clown Himself and therefore indulges in carnivalizing the world. Isn't the spectacle of a Jewish boy, praying like a Catholic in a cathedral until his girlfriend returns with a contraceptive device, evidence enough that Neil might not be altogether blasphemous?

7 David Schearl in the Polyphonic World

In her interview with Henry Roth, Bonnie Lyons, who was to make the virtually definitive study of *Call It Sleep*, was intent on eliciting from her subject an affirmative view of David Schearl's life and, indeed, of the world in general.[1] Quoting Roth's comment that "the impressionable boy living in hostile surroundings adopts as his own a destructive act to which he is instigated by outsiders to whom he has no personal relationship," she asks, "Doesn't David transform that destructive act into a positive act?" (They are talking about the climactic event, in which David disrupts the electrical system of a streetcar line by plunging a metal implement between the tracks into the third rail.) "At the time," Roth replies, "I thought this was a beautiful symbol of power destroying—what? The child was symbolically destroyed although he lived on. Something was destroyed in him, I don't know exactly what—perhaps his flights of fancy, the artist in him, perhaps it was childhood." "But the vision was positive," insists Lyons. And Roth answers, "He does feel a sense of triumph. I don't know what he feels triumph about. At this stage of the game, if you ask me, I couldn't tell you. The only thing I think that he feels triumphant about . . . was that for one brief second he was able to summon something up that unified the world. . . .

It is not the way a true unification is attained." This is still not enough for Lyons, who continues, "Although the world is not purified, doesn't David have a private, internal transformation?"

> Roth: Well, I think so.
> [Lyons]: Even though he has to return to the "fallen world"?
> Roth: The sense of triumph he feels in the end was that he made the attempt, even though it is a failure.... Even if it does not succeed, the martyr cannot be deprived of the feeling that he made the attempt—even if he shows that this is wrong, that this is not the way to do it. (170–171)

This is the reply not of a true believer but of a skeptic; it does not confirm Lyons' view that Roth is, after all is said and done, an optimist, but that he is at best an ambivalent witness to the conduct or ethos of his characters.

From beginning to end the story of David Schearl is that of the failure of a hypersensitive child, driven by fear and feelings of guilt, to obtain the knowledge, secular or divine, that he craves. While the ways he follows are Jewish ones, they do not lead to Jewish conclusions, and none of God's Names is ever revealed to him.

David's obsession with Isaiah, which came into being while he listened to the rabbi's running commentary as a classmate bungled his way through a chanting of the Torah, is typical of his responses to the world around him. Confronted with the sight of the Almighty and "His terrible light," Isaiah becomes aware of his own uncleanliness:

> "But just when Isaiah let out this cry—I am unclean—one of the angels flew to the altar and with tongs drew out a fiery coal.... And with that coal, down he flew to Isaiah and with that coal touched his lips—Here! ... You are clean! And the instant that coal touched Isaiah's lips, then he heard God's own voice say, Whom shall I send? Who will go for us? And Isaiah spoke and—" (227)

But the rabbi is interrupted and David is left with enough questions to keep him obsessed for a long time to come. He will wonder, for instance, where one goes to speak to God; whether the coal used to purify Isaiah was white instead of black; why he wasn't clean in the first place. These questions are typical of the way in which his curiosity about the world in general is expressed. Although his mother overwhelms him with love and protection, she does not always satisfy his inquisitiveness. He needs what Buber might call a partner-in-dialogue; what he finds is isolation and the constant fear his lack of knowledge brings to him.[2]

Still, certain things about the world are revealed to him, partially if not wholly, and they are revealed in a special way. The episode in which he eavesdrops on his mother as she relates to her sister the story of her secret romance reflects his unending struggle with words and meanings. To begin with, she speaks in Polish, "that alien, aggravating tongue that David could never fathom"; but she still uses a few Yiddish words and phrases that come through to him "like mica-glints in the sidewalk." "When would another phrase break from that alien thicket?" he asks. Then, as she lapses into Yiddish,

> her voice took on a throbbing richness that David had never heard in it before. The very sound seemed to reverberate in his flesh sending pulse after pulse of a nameless tingling excitement through his body. (260)

But,

> with the same suddenness as before, meaning scaled the horizon to another idiom, leaving David stranded on a sounding but empty shore. Words here and there, phrases shimmering like distant sails tantalized him, but never drew near.

So that,

[he] inwardly writhed at his own impotence.

It seemed to him. . . . that his mind would fly apart if he brought no order to this confusion. . . . But still the phrases flickered on as ephemeral and capricious as before, as thwarting—the abrupt and fragmentary glimpses of a figure passing behind the brief notches of parapets.

The tale of illicit romance with a gentile that Genya reveals to her sister, Bertha, can scarcely be appreciated by her seven-year-old son and would not have been even had it been told all in Yiddish. David's epistemological agonies, like those of the mystic who is not yet sufficiently purified to receive authentic illumination, leave him only with fragmentary knowledge, the hints of order and meaning shining through the chaos of ignorance.

But important, too, in this experience is the ecstasy of rhythm, beyond meaning, beyond conventional knowledge. "Her voice took on a throbbing richness" and the "very sound" sends "pulse after pulse" reverberating through his body. This is similar to the ecstasy he feels when reading the Torah in a Hebrew that he can pronounce but the meaning of which (the *chumish* or translation) he cannot fathom. And Hebrew, we recall, is the sacred, mysterious language, the Logos embodied by the Torah and the story of Isaiah in particular.

In the chaos and cacophony of the *cheder*, Hebrew is lost amid the babble of the unruly students:

A seething of whispers began to chafe the room.
"You hea' me say it. You hea' me! Shid on you. . . ."
"Said whom shall I send?" The rabbi's words were baffling on the thick briars of sound. "Who will go for us?"
"Izzy Pissy! Cock-eye Mulligan! Mah nishtanah halilaw hazeh—
"Wanna play me Yonk?"

The uproar continues unabated until the rabbi explodes and metes out corporal punishment. But he is not long in singling out David as a favorite because of his ability to read the Torah rapidly and as though he understands it, even though in fact he doesn't understand a word.

By the time he is asked to perform for a visiting rabbi, David has an obvious feeling for the Torah, a sense of the rhythm that, like his mother's voice, pulsates within him, pointing to but never actually revealing a transcendent meaning. Again, and this time with a more obvious significance, it is the Isaiah episode, now in its continuation, that the teacher picks out. The Hebrew emerges from the text, not as it does when it is usually recited by students—in a drone, like "syllables pulled from a drab and tedious reel"—but as it was meant to sound: "a chant, a hymn, as though a soaring presence behind the words pulsed and stressed a meaning. . . . "Shaish kenawfayim shash kenawfayim leahod. . . . The words, forms of immense grandeur behind a cloudy screen, overwhelmed him. . ." (497).

God is the presence who pulses a meaning (Logos), not one that David can grasp but, because he is not wholly "present" (to recall Buber), can only sense. Isaiah's story is, in essence, completed when, purified, he can speak out to accept God's appointment as His prophet; but it is not completed for David, who is still a child, still filled with confusion and fear, guilt and anxiety. In this climactic episode he is also so distracted by recent events and what he has divined of his mother's old secret that he fabricates a story claiming that his real mother is dead and that an impostor has taken her place.

There are no definitive visions of a transcendent, or even an ideal, secular reality in *Call It Sleep*, a novel, which, if it takes any position at all, it is that of the ambivalence or ambiguity of things, events, persons, and life itself. Family life in particular is hard, especially when dominated by a man like Albert Schearl, whose hatred for his enemies, both real and imagined, is exceeded only by that for his wife and son. The classrooms and playgrounds of the *cheder* can be as menacing as those of the public school, and the Jewish street gangs scarcely seem any kinder to David that the anti-Semitic ones. That David's world is not devoid of signs and wonders is both his consolation and tragedy; what they have to tell him, though sometimes dazzling, is always equivocal. The mystical moment of candle-lighting by his mother that ushers in the Sabbath, the deep tranquillity afforded by the summer sky seen from the tenement roof, the instant of exaltation before oblivion that David experiences when he taps the power source are all signs that he looks to "relieve his watchfulness and forever insure his well-being."

In the power surge that erupts from below the tracks there is all the aura and force of revelation, but, as revelation wholly devoid of Logos, it speaks nothing to anyone: "Like a paw ripping through the sable fibres of the earth, power, gigantic, fetterless, thudded into day! And light, unleashed, terrific light bellowed out of iron lips. . . ." In a pagan society or one without faith in God "signs are taken for wonders" and the Logos of Hebrew is lost in the babble (Babel) of the exploitive relations that characterize the modern world. Meaning, order, the confirmation of being should be fulfilled, as Buber would put it, in the "interhuman" region in which authentic dialogue takes place. The wholeness of speech in Logos reflects the wholeness of men who, having turned toward one another in meeting, establish a partnership-in-dialogue. Conversely, behind the fragments of speech that mark human discourse, the fractured babel of the many dialects of ethnic English that flow through the concluding section of *Call It Sleep*, there may or may not be a Presence; neither Roth nor his character—nor the reader—can tell. Analogous to the polyphonic linguistic world described by Bakhtin, it is a world in which no single voice—neither of God nor author—prevails and each person speaks a mono-logos of his or her own. Specifically, that means diatribe, threat, imprecation, and abuse, until finally the world becomes a polyglot of voices, detached from person and babbling inanities.

2. The Monological Jew in Fiction

In the final lines of the novel, however, Roth does present what seems to be both a theory of the novel and an affirmation of life. In moving toward sleep, he says, the mind responds to images thrown up by memory far more sensitively than when fully awake:

> It was only toward sleep that every wink of the eyelids could strike a spark into the cloudy tinder of the dark, kindle out of shadowy corners of the bedroom such myriad and such vivid jets of images—of the glint on tilted beards, of the uneven shine on roller skates, of the dry light on gray stone steps, of the tapering glitter of rails, of the oily sheen on the night-smooth rivers, of the glow on thin blond hair. . . .

The ears also respond:

> the hoarse voice, the scream of fear, the bells, the thick-breathing, the roar of crowds and all sounds that lie fermenting in the vats of silence and the past. . . .

And finally the sense of touch or contact:

> one knew himself still lying on the cobbles under him, and over him and scudding ever toward him like a black foam, the perpetual blur of shod and running feet, the broken shoes, new shoes . . . under skirts, under trousers, shoes. . . . and feel them all and feel, not pain, not terror, but strangest triumph, strangest acquiescence.

All of these images are associated with a single event—the power surge and display of sparks and light that David had set off, nearly killing himself. It is significant that here, at the end of his story, the climactic episode should come to him not as a single and unified vision but as a fragmentary rush of highly distinct and sharply perceived images. This is the Imagist way of perceiving reality; its triumph is, and must be, aesthetic, not epistemological, just as David's acquiescence must be in a life sensed but never understood. Thus *Call It Sleep* does not end in despair even though the Burning Bush has become a gratuitous explosion of light and power and Moses has become a strange, bemused child only partly literate in the language of an almighty but conspicuously absent God.

8   Levinsky and the Language of Acquisition

What does the rise in *The Rise of David Levinsky* actually mean? We know what it means in *The Rise of Silas Lapham* by that author whom Abraham Cahan admired as a realist, William Dean Howells, but the question of Cahan's attitude toward his hero is more complex and more fraught with ambiguity. Even though Levinsky is in many ways a projection of his creator and often serves as his spokesman, the novel is far from being autobiographical. For one thing, the author was a life-long socialist, the character a business tycoon, portrayed as having, whatever his faults, a great deal of sensitivity and insight.

Why has Cahan chosen, in his one important novel, to omit the struggles of the Jewish socialist movement in America, in which he himself played no mean part, and instead to concentrate on the personal problems of a single, bourgeois man—to take as his central concern not the class struggle in the period of rapid industrialization after the Civil War but the vicissitudes in the life of an ambitious but essentially nonpolitical Russian immigrant?[1] His reading of Plekhanov, Marx, and Engels, not to mention his personal experiences as a propagandist and agitator, does not shape with any real consistency Cahan's conception of the virtues and flaws of American society or his view of the life of the Jewish immigrant.

Atheistic socialism and monotheistic Judaism have, perhaps, a common denominator in the belief that self-fulfillment is possible only in social terms, in contrast with individualistically centered theories, which state that perfectability lies only with the single man and that self-fulfillment cannot be transcended. David Levinsky is neither a socialist nor, in his adulthood, a Torah-reading Jew; he is philosophically, as well as literally, on his own. He must, in essence, create his own values or at least act without any sanction of authority or possibility of confirmation. His values and ideals are therefore an assemblage drawn from the various layers of his experience and they ultimately satisfy psychic needs rather than claim universality.

It is precisely the preoccupation with language—with the perpetual confrontation, encounter, or meeting expressed in and by dialogue—that makes the theories of Martin Buber so valuable as a perspective on Cahan's novel. The world of individuality—the existential world in which the predatory Other and the I-It relations among men prevail—appears here in sharp definition. It is a world that Cahan cannot condemn or exonerate, neither rebel against as militant socialist or disillusioned Jew nor wholly embrace.

Whatever its defects, America is the Golden Land and that faith underlies and is expressed in this outburst in a Catskill resort during a dinner concert (Levinsky is caught up in the emotion and so, we can assume from the absence of irony, is Cahan, himself):

> [The audience has joined in with the playing of the "Star Spangled Banner"] Men and women were offering thanksgiving to the flag under which they were eating this good dinner, wearing these expensive clothes. There was the jingle of newly-acquired dollars in our applause. But there was something else in it as well. . . . It was as if they were saying: "We are not persecuted under this flag. At last we have found a home."
>
> Love for America blazed up in my soul. . . . we all sang the anthem from the bottom of our souls. (424)

2. The Monological Jew in Fiction

I do not think it is coincidental that Thackeray should be mentioned as one of Levinsky's favorite writers, for Levinsky's world, if not one of upheaval in the socialist sense, is a Vanity Fair in which the struggle for survival is carried out with chiefly verbal weapons and nothing succeeds like eloquence.

Now, Buber classifies dialogue into three forms, the last of which is of particular interest to us here.[2] I shall not insist that the description is applicable in all its technical details to Cahan's novel, but it does give us an insight into the relation between speech and character when the ideal cannot be reached. Buber calls the first variant *debate* and says that in this form,

> thoughts are not expressed as they existed in the mind but in speaking are so pointed that they may strike home in the sharpest way, and moreover *without the men that are spoken to being regarded in any way present as persons;* [then there is] *conversation* characterized by the need neither to communicate something, nor to learn something, nor to influence someone, nor to come into connexion with someone, but solely by the desire to have one's self-reliance confirmed by marking the impression that is made, or if it has become unsteady to have it strengthened. (19–20, my italics)

Buber concludes the list with "friendly chat," in which each speaker regards himself as an absolute and the other as relative, and lovers' talk, in which each partner enjoys only his own soul and "precious experience." I do not propose, at this point, to seek out passages in the novel that best illustrate these categories. I'm sure very few would exist in the pure state. They are most useful when taken suggestively rather than literally. Monologue disguised as dialogue is, I daresay, the primary expression of the moral vulnerability of the fictive America that Cahan has created and peopled.

"We are all actors, more or less," says Levinsky. "The question is only what our aim is, and whether we are capable of a 'convincing personation' " (194). This principle underlies social discourse in a culture founded upon competition, and competition not just for material gain or "success" but for psychological and spiritual fulfillment as well. The real crisis of dialogue in Levinsky's America does not stem from the simple antagonism of material and spiritual values; it stems from bringing spiritual values under the aegis of the principles of acquisition. Thus Levinsky is neither morally nor culturally insensitive; he fully recognizes the values of education, family life, religion, art—indeed, without them, he has found that, despite all his commercial success, his life is empty and lonely. His yearning for love and a family eventually outweighs his financial ambition, though he never captures the happiness he so avidly pursues. Like the pursuit of love or God, the pursuit of happiness is fraught with deception and contradiction. Manifested in dialogue, it reveals or yields nothing more than the vanity of the speaker, his inability to transcend the logic and rhetoric of materialism, and thereby his definitive failure to attain the wholeness and communion with another that he seeks throughout a lifetime.

Consider the episode in which, desperate for cash to hire a talented designer that can make his cloak factory prosper, Levinsky approaches an old girl friend, Gussie, to ask for a loan. The conversation, held in a quiet place in a park, rapidly turns into a "fencing contest" in which Gussie, stung before by Levinsky, smartly counters all his arguments. Midway through, Levinsky finds himself being carried away by the beauty of the spring night and the sounds of a nearby band:

> We fell silent, both of us, listening to the singing. Poor Gussie! She was not a pretty girl, and she did not interest me in the least. Yet at this moment I was drawn to her. The brooding plaintive tones.... filled me with yearning ... filled me with love. Gussie was a woman to me now. My hand sought hers. It was an honest proffer of endearment, for my soul was praying for communion with hers. (198)

"An honest proffer of endearment"—as though endearment were a commodity over which one entered into negotiations. And although the religious rhetoric of "My soul was praying . . ." is sincere, its very sincerity betrays a shallow idea about the true meanings of "soul," "praying," and "communion," all of which Levinsky has trivialized by associating them with what he admits are "temporary" feelings. "I swear to you you're dear to me," he argues, forgetting that if she really were dear to him, he wouldn't have to "swear" to the fact. But the lady yields and there follows, sure enough, a "delirium of love-making" (passionate embraces and kisses) at the conclusion of which both are left sober and depressed. That Levinsky had at one point been ready to marry Gussie all the more underscores his confusion of motives. Whether spiritual or material, all things are to be attained by the techniques of acquisition. Even the genuine intimacy of an I-Thou relation is diluted by exploitation as the it, to which the Thou is more and more reduced, begins to emerge. The subject is no longer regarded as a whole human being and a "partner-in-dialogue" but as an object to be pursued and acquired.[3]

Levinsky's real attitude toward Gussie is one of condescension and pity, and there is little room left for genuine love or even romance. His relation with Dora Margolis, wife of his friend Max, is another matter. Whatever the sincerity of his love—indeed all the more so because of it—Levinsky never stops calculating. Attempting to seduce Dora, he slips into Yiddish, a language regarded as being suitable only for personal or family matters. It's not that he is fundamentally apathetic toward her as he was to Gussie; we can believe him when he says, "I really loved her." On the other hand, he knows all too well exactly what he is doing:

> "Dearest," I whispered.
> "I must go out," she said. . . .
> "Don't. Don't go away from me, Dora. Please don't," I said in Yiddish, with the least bit of authority. "I love thee. I love thee, Dora," I raved, for the first time addressing her

in the familiar pronoun.... "Dost thou love me Dora? Tell me. I want to hear it from thine own lips."

This appeal ends in a kiss that sends Levinsky into ecstasy. But is it physical or spiritual ecstasy—lust or love, thrill of conquest or intimacy, egocentricity or genuine sharing with another? These are the very questions that Levinsky was capable of asking himself:

> My heart was dancing for joy over my conquest of her, and at the same time I felt that I was almost ready to lay down my life for her. It was a blend of animal selfishness and spiritual sublimity. I really loved her. (278–79)

It will remain a "blend" until Levinsky is able to give himself without there being anything for him to pursue and acquire—until no longer wanting anything, he ceases "personation," and speaks to the lady in his own voice and in his wholeness as a human being. Circumstances, however, will not let him break the pattern. In regard to Max Margolis, Dora's husband, with whom he wishes to keep cordial relations, he tells us:

> I consulted Max, as I did quite often now. Not that I thought myself in need of his advice, or anyone else's, for that matter.... I played the intimate and ardent friend, and this was simply part of my personation. (290)

Levinsky may seem close to entering into a "dialogical event" with Meyer Nodelman, who, he says,

> was a most attractive man to talk to, especially when the conversation dealt with one's intimate life. With all his illiteracy and crudity of language he had rare insight into the human heart and was full of subtle sympathy. He was the only person in America with whom I often indulged in a heart-to-heart confab. (357)

It is to his credit that Levinsky recognizes that "crudity

of language" can be as valuable as, if not more than, the eloquence with which he himself invariably speaks. Ironically, Nodelman, recognizing Levinsky's loneliness, tries unsuccessfully to act as a marriage broker for him and leaves Levinsky no better off than he was. The more he seeks an escape from the materialist and philistine world, the more confirmed he becomes in his acquisitive habits: "I had no creed, I knew of no ideals. The only thing I believed in was the cold, drab theory of the struggle for existence and the survival of the fittest."

This is, of course, not enough for Levinsky (we have heard him say things like this before) and he tells us: "This could not satisfy a heart that was hungry for enthusiasm and affection, so dreams of family life became my religion. Self-sacrificing devotion to one's family was the only kind of altruism and idealism I did not flout." If we are suspicious of such a declaration, it is with good reason, for Levinsky continues:

> I was worth over a million, and my profits had reached enormous dimensions, so I was regarded as a most desirable match, and match-makers pestered me as much as I would let them, but they found me a hard man to suit. (380–81)

The assumption here is simply that old cliché that money can buy anything, a family no less than a factory—and that money coupled with eloquence are the main implements for acquiring whatever one yearns for or dreams of. Levinsky tries to perform his "public duty" in the same way and describes his philanthropic activity, proudly citing that he gave so much that they put his picture in the newspaper. Vanity is so obviously mixed with altruism here, we don't know whether to praise his efforts or decry their motives.

Levinsky's narration reveals that his rise was to wealth and a greater awareness of the refinements of American civilization and human nature, in general. It also reveals that the very elements that gave him his wealth and led to a certain sophistication are the ones that kept that sophistication limited and subverted his sense of values. Wooing Anna Tevkin, the daughter of a well-known but now neglected poet, he shows us how little he has learned about the love and family life that he has never stopped pursuing:

> I loved her to insanity. She was the supreme desire of my being. [This does not assure us of Levinsky's maturity, nor, considering his expectations, does it bode well for the lady who is the object of all this supercharged feeling.] I knew that she was weaker in character and mind than Elsie, for example, but that seemed to be a point in her favor. [A point in her favor to be of weaker character and mind? This is not the case of man and woman entering into an I-Thou relation as partners-in-dialogue and other, more physical, forms of communication; it is the precondition of an I-It relation, in which the woman tries to be whatever her husband's values dictate that she should be.] "She is a good girl," I would muse, "mild, kindly, girlish." As for her 'radical' notions, "they really don't matter much. I could easily knock them out of her. I should be happy with her. Oh, how happy!" [Is comment necessary?] (482–83)

Levinsky's assumptions about marital relations, about women as a whole, and about Anna Tevkin in particular are perfectly in keeping with his assumptions about the way of life in America. His egoism, his chauvinism, the materialism by which he measures all things are not an eccentricity but representative of an entire society. In his own way Levinsky has succeeded in assimilating where so many others (like Stern, for example) have failed.

His is not a story of the contradictions of being a Jew in America. True, Levinsky clings to Judaism and from time to time goes to temple. He longs for the old days when he read Talmud, but this is mere nostalgia, for his actual practice of Judaism is a matter of philanthropy and has little to do with any spiritual belief. He suffers no crisis of faith on his way to becoming an American and experiences very little anti-Semitism to test his belief. Here is how he resolves the age-old problem:

> [The cloth merchant] was well disposed toward me.... he addressed me as Dave. (There was a note of condescension as well as of admiration in this "Dave" of his. It implied that I was a shrewd fellow and an excellent customer, singularly successful and reliable, but that I was his inferior, all the same—a Jew, a social pariah. At the bottom of my heart I considered myself his superior, finding an amusing discrepancy between his professorial face and the crudity of his intellectual interests; *but he was a Gentile and an American, and a much wealthier man than I, so I looked up to him.*) (501–2, my italics)

Thus, after scoffing at the cloth merchant for thinking him inferior, Levinsky reverts to the same anti-Semitic logic and ends up agreeing with him. And he can agree with him precisely because anti-Semitism is not an important factor in his life. It enters the narration only once again—in the episode in which Levinsky gives up any idea of marrying a gentile woman with whom he has much in common, because he is frightened by that "medieval prejudice against our people which makes so many marriages between Jew and Gentile a failure." But Levinsky gets over this loss with little grief just as he gets over the loss of all the Jewish women with whom he sought matrimony. His real agony comes from "loneliness" and that is a hazard of individualism in general and not an evil experienced just by exiled Jews.

In other words, Levinsky is not alone in his loneliness; he is lonely because he lives by the values of a society atomized by competition—a society oriented to the marketplace and not the hearth. His tragedy is that, though desperate in his loneliness to enter the hearth, he cannot do so without bringing the values of the marketplace with him.

9 The Family Moskat's Descent into Randomness

"I spin and I spin and nothing comes out of it," says Meshulam Moskat, patriarch of the family whose three generations are the subject of I. B. Singer's epic novel:

> "I've had two wives, seven children, given out dowries, supported sons-in-law. It's cost me millions! And what have I got out of it? A bunch of enemies, gluttons, parasites. A fine generation I've spawned." (88)

Meshulam is speaking here to his third wife, Rosa Frumetl, and her replies are less than satisfactory:

> "Meshulam, it's a sin to talk that way."
> "Let it be a sin. As long as I've got a tongue I'll speak, and if God wants to lash me for it, it'll be my behind that gets the whip, not yours."

He resumes his lament but this time he seems to realize his own culpability in the matter:

> That my children are worthless . . . is nobody's fault. I myself am a hard man, stubborn, spiteful, something of a villain. I don't deny it.

2. The Monological Jew in Fiction

How hard and stubborn a man he is is evidenced by the very conversation he is holding with Rosa Frumetl, which is not a conversation at all—not, as it should be, an intimate dialogue between partners—but simply a monologue in which the speaker's tongue alone is in control:

> "Meshulam, what kind of talk is this?" Rosa Frumetl broke in.
> "Quiet, woman! I'm not talking to you. I'm talking to the wall," Meshulam rumbled.

For all the help Rosa Frumetl has given him, Meshulam might as well have been talking to the wall; but it is clear that no matter how she replied, he would still be talking only to the wall because that is all he is capable of doing. "All is vanity and vexation of spirit," he later reflects. And vanity is the isolating egoism that has made Meshulam a rich man and pillar of the Jewish community of Warsaw and at the same time contributed to his ultimate loneliness and deathbed despair. The disintegration of the family Moskat begins with its founder; its causes, forms, and significance as revealed in his progeny is Singer's main concern in the saga that may well be his masterpiece.

Although the Moskats, as exemplified by Meshulam, give every sign of being observant Jews, their Judaism, little more than a matter of performing rituals and holiday ceremonies, holds almost no sway over their feelings, ideas, or conduct. It merely masks the strife, bitterness, and resentment that mark the true character of family relationships. Disaffected from grandchildren no less than his own children, Meshulam condemns the so-called modern Jews and the chaos and incomprehensibility they have brought into his life; and even though he sees himself as partly to blame for what has happened, he does so for the wrong reasons:

> He regretted everything now: that he had twice married daughters of undistinguished families and spawned chil-

dren of no accomplishments; that he had not been more discriminating in the choice of sons-in-law; that he had made such a fool of himself as to marry for a third time. ... (193)

As a microcosm of Polish Jewry in the Diaspora, the family Moskat suffers the rebellion of the generations, its young, lured by the values of Western culture, specifically modern Polish society. As one member of the family, Pinnie, who has remained within the Hasidic fold, reflects:

> "Old Meshulam Moskat had been a king among Jews; and with all their faults, his sons had managed to stay Jews. But the grandchildren had completely alienated themselves from the old ways. . . . More than twenty years had gone by since old Moskat had died, and the Jewish kingdom over which he had ruled . . . had long been in ruins." (551)

The crumbling authority of the family, the weakening influence of Jewish moral beliefs, the lessening faith in God and Torah have all been accompanied by a rising individualism that inevitably expresses itself in terms of self-gratification—the pursuit of pleasure (chiefly by adultery) and material wealth. Thus the family Moskat gradually ceases to function as a group and becomes atomized into independently striving, personally ambitious individuals, so that what old forms survive cannot contain the anarchy of emotions, loyalties, affections, desires, and passions in which most of the characters are caught up.

Miserable until the day he dies, Meshulam looks vainly for the meaning of things. He looks, however, not into himself but into the sky—for a sign in the changing clouds and sunset:

> A hand made out of light, mist, and space was weaving and darting, making intricate patterns, writing some secret message. But what it all meant no ordinary son of man

could hope to understand. Would he, Meshulam Moskat, at least find the truth of things at the other side? (193)

Meshulam's vision of meaningless patterns in the sky reminds us of David Schearl's; and in Singer's world, as in Henry Roth's, life, always its mysterious self, yields no revelation, no final logos to human knowledge or moral law for human conduct. One's acts carry their own reward or punishment.

Although Singer obviously has a moral position in regard to his characters, it often seems that as author he adopts the guise of the God of Spinoza in whom every idea is true—inadequate and confused ones no less than those that are adequate and clear. I am alluding here to a passage, taken out of context, in which one of the main characters, Asa Heshel Bannet, is trying to justify his own false reflections or inadequate ideas (555).

Roughly speaking, Spinoza's pantheistic deity, conceived of as being coterminous with nature or reality, is an appropriate paradigm for the kind of "individualism" that Asa Heshel practices in contrast to the monotheistic deity who, envisioned in his anthropomorphism as the Father, is an appropriate paradigm for the whole conception of marriage and family. In any case it is in Asa Heshel that Singer portrays the kind of individualism that marks the ruin of the "Jewish kingdom" ruled by Meshulam.[1] Asa Heshel is a "modern Jew," a once ambitious Talmudic scholar who comes to Warsaw to make his fortune, falls in love with one of Meshulam's granddaughters, Hadassah, and eventually turns into an intellectual and spiritual drifter. Having virtually abandoned the Mosaic Law, he has the moral and philosophical freedom of the existential man, and like the existential man he cannot commit that freedom to person, thing, or cause; that includes Hadassah, whom he overcomes great difficulties to marry (both have spouses they do not love) only to experience increasing apathy and mutual hostility. His life filled with "purposeless brooding,

The Family Moskat

fantasies, unquenched passions," he has, in "his chase after pleasure . . . neglected everything—his health, his relatives, his work, his career" (561). "I'm killing myself," he reflects,

> But why, why? Because I have no faith. That minimum of faith without which one cannot exist. . . . But how can I rescue myself? In what can I believe? I hate God, I hate Him and His creation. How can one love a dead God, a paper God? I am *kaput, kaput*. (536)

Regarded from Martin Buber's standpoint, Asa Heshel's condition has its own fatal logic. Unlike Abram Shapiro, who enjoys his vices and dies affirming himself a Jew, Asa Heshel, despite his pursuit of women, is a born ascetic and suffers most when he should be most enjoying himself. His failure in human relations is a failure of *responsibility*—or response to address by another. "How can one love a dead God?" he asks and that is exactly the point. God is dead for him because the world, creation, is dead. As Buber argues in his critique of Kierkegaard ("Question to the Single One"), God is not man's rival. Kierkegaard had asserted that in order to love, he had to remove the object, Regina Olsen, whom after a long courtship he refused to marry. He was wrong, Buber says. Far from loving God exclusively, man is able to love him only through his creatures. Every I requires a Thou:

> Only when I have to do with another essentially, that is, in such a way that he is no longer a phenomenon of my *I*, but instead is my *Thou*, do I experience the reality of speech with another—in the irrefragable genuineness of mutuality. (*Between Man and Man*, 50–51)

Thus for Buber "speaking with God is something *toto genere* different from 'speaking with oneself'; whereas, remarkably, it is not something *toto genere* different from speaking with another human being."

Aside from his mercurial romance with Hadassah—and

even here it is dubious—only twice in the novel does Asa Heshel find a genuinely intimate moment with another, genuine insofar as his response/responsibility is genuine. One is with his infant son, David:

> A sudden love welled up in him for this cross youngster. In that instant he realized for the first time the meaning of the words 'to be a father.' "I mustn't," he thought. "I daren't bind myself to him. She'll [Adele, his first wife] never stop blackmailing me." He bent down and kissed little David on the forehead.
> "David, darling, I'm your daddy. I love you. . . ."

This is not exactly what Buber would call a dialogical event, but it is as close to one as Asa Heshel can come. Here the gesture is worth a thousand words. And curiously it is the same gesture, a kiss bestowed on the forehead, that marks one of the few moments of selfless intimacy between adults in this saga of strife-ridden men and women. Significantly, it is a moment that is as gratuitous as the sudden access of love in Asa Heshel for his son, coming as it does after an exchange in which Asa Heshel's attempt to unburden himself to the dying Abram Shapiro is met with mock irony:

> "A fine thing! Here I am on my deathbed, and I have to comfort him. The end of the world hasn't come yet."
> "The end of our world *has* come."
> "You're a lunatic. You've let yourself fall into a melancholy. What do you want to do? Sit down and weep?"
> "Personally, I can't take it anymore. . . ."
> "Shut up! You're not letting me die in peace. Tell me, exactly, what is it you want to do? Get converted?"

But beneath Abram's sniping there is apparently a depth of feeling for Asa Heshel that belies his gruff words:

> Abram's large, dark eyes gazed steadily at him from behind the heavy brows. The crease in his forehead deepened, like a wound. After a while he dropped his head back on the pillows and closed his lids. He lay motionless. Then he opened one eye. "Come and kiss me."
> Asa Heshel bent over the bed and kissed Abram on the brow. Abram raised his arms and put them around Asa Heshel's shoulders. "I believe in God," he murmured. "I die a Jew." (535)

Notice that it is not speech that carries this transcendent moment but simply gesture—and it is enough for both men. Abram has embraced God by embracing Asa Heshel. We don't know what is going on inside Asa Heshel's head at this point, for Singer gives him neither speech nor response that goes beyond the act. It is entirely possible that he is not destined to repeat Abram's words and that the gesture is nothing more than itself, and that wordless men, believing in neither God nor man, cannot die Jews.

Part Three
False Gods, Graven Images

10 Art and Idolatry

We do not have to determine the symbolism of the golden calf to appreciate its significance in the history of the Jews. It needs no symbolism to give it meaning; it need only be what it is, a thing, an object, an idol. Created by circumstances—the "children of Israel" have grown restless over Moses' prolonged absence on Sinai—it answers, though poorly, the need to find a protective deity. As we all know, it brings down the wrath of God, who despite his word to Moses, commands that all the sinners be killed, a number, we are told, that reaches three thousand. In many ways responsible for this cataclysm, Moses' brother Aaron, whom God made the prophet of Moses, just as Moses was the prophet of God, tries to tell what happened when the people demanded that he "make us gods, which shall go before us":

> And Aaron said unto them, "Break off the golden earrings, which are in the ears of your wives, of your sons, and of your daughters, and bring them unto me."
> And all the people broke off all the golden earrings which were in their ears, and brought them unto Aaron.
> And he received them at their hand, and fashioned it with

3. False Gods, Graven Images

a graving tool, after he had made it a molten calf: and they said, "These be thy gods, O Israel."

Now, in every way this event is a profane analogue to the apocalyptic occurrence then taking place on Mt. Sinai. "And the Lord spoke unto Moses face to face, as a man speaketh unto his friend." This dialogue, signifying the ultimate I-Thou relation, is possible because Moses' faith in God is unshakable and God's confidence in Moses is almost unlimited. Each is *present* to the other; that is, each, fully aware of his own and the Other's wholeness, is prepared to enter into this meeting (even though God, whose logic is not always known to man, later warns that "Thou canst not see my face: for there shall no man see me, and live"). These are the circumstances under which Moses receives God's Law, inscribed on stone tablets, and returns with them.

In replacing God with gods and their idols the people have given up an I-Thou relation, and all the meaning it entails, for a relation hopelessly limited to the I-It. There is no dialogue with an object, no transcendent meaning or authority expressed in a golden calf. It is nothing more than matter given shape by the artisan's tool, a puny reflection of the Living God's creation of the universe. Unlike God's appeal to the whole person—and only God in his singularity can appeal to the totality of a person in his or her singularity—the appeal of the golden calf is to the senses alone. It is, in effect, a certain kind of artwork: one that presumes to be an end in itself and to exist for its own sake. We call it the religion of art and in Jewish eyes it is a throwback to paganism.

In Cynthia Ozick's work we find the broadest application of the second commandment and probably the most inclusive statement on what constitutes idolatry in the modern world. "Most inclusive" but not "final"; we are not going to be finished with the issue of false gods and graven images until we have again looked to Martin Buber.

Art and Idolatry

Ozick, whose essays are no less sophisticated than her fiction, tells us that idols in Mosaic thought are anything "that is allowed to come between ourselves and God. Anything that is *instead of* God. Anything that we call an end in itself, and yet is not God" (*Art and Ardor*, 207). Coming under this definition is the religion of art, in which form and language have been glorified. What Ozick calls "aesthetic paganism" is a form of idolatry that has isolated the Jewish writer, who alone is "indifferent to aesthetics" and alone wants to "passionately wallow in human reality." For the Jew, she tells us, "covenant and conduct are above decoration" (165), and the literature he creates is (or ideally will be) "liturgical" and make its appeal to a public rather than to a coterie.

We are not far here from Buber, who says in *The Knowledge of Man* that man's confrontation with things that he puts into words and thereby raises to their full status as things is not "decisive." What is decisive is men's coming to an understanding over situations. "*Not things but situations are primary*" (116, my italics).

This sounds like humanism but it does not answer all our questions, the main one being, In what way can the perception of objects be adjudged a human act and a part of the very reality in which Ozick tells us that the Jewish writer is constrained to wallow? Can the object be dissociated from the idol and the Jew morally allowed to proceed as an "objectivist"? This question leads us straight into the complexities of Buber's view of man's relation to things and to the Hasidism that inspired it.

"Not things but situations are primary." Well and good, but this does not mean that man's relation to things is not crucial to his relation to God:

> God can be beheld in each thing and reached through each pure deed. . . . the least thing in the world is worthy that through it God should reveal Himself to the man who truly seeks Him. (*Hasidism and Modern Man*, 49)

3. False Gods, Graven Images

That is to say,

> no thing can exist without a divine spark, and each person can uncover and redeem this spark at each time and through each action, even the most ordinary, if only he performs it in purity. . . .

Thus, Buber concludes,

> One must serve God with one's whole life, with the whole of the everyday, with the whole of reality. The salvation of man does not lie in his holding himself far removed from the worldly, but in consecrating it to holy, to divine meaning. . . . It lies in his preserving the great love of God for all creatures, yes, for all things. (50)

This is not entirely different from Whitman's view of the universe; nor is it far from William Carlos Williams' "egalitarian" aesthetic—that is, if we eliminate the theology. But if we do eliminate it, aren't we revealing ourselves, in the eyes of the monotheist (Jewish tradition, in other words), to be idol worshippers, embracing creation but not the creator, hallowing the object but not for the sake of the "Single One"? In this case the word "idolatry" has only metaphoric and not literal value, just as the idols (images) and "false gods" in Williams' mythopoeia (*Paterson*) rule (though badly) only the linguistic universe of an allegorical poem.

Buber doesn't speak of idolatry per se, but in his aesthetic theory he both substantiates and adds a philosophical dimension to Ozick's view. He begins by positing the object as a Kantian ding-an-sich, an existent, an x unconditioned by any human qualities. Through man's perception the object appears in the world in all its color, shape, and texture—a process of figuration by which man discovers or invents meaning in the substance of things. But like all animals, asserts Buber, man sees only what he wants to see; perception-figuration is limited to human needs and uses in an "I-It" relationship.

Art and Idolatry

There is, however, something that "goes beyond" need and function, something that can be grasped only by vision, the artist's figuration that "transcends need and makes the superfluous into the necessary." Unlike the observer, who is concerned with fixing the observed in his mind, with noting him, the "onlooker" (and "all great artists have been onlookers") sees the object "freely, and undisturbed awaits what will be presented to him" (*Between Man and Man*, 8, 9). Uninterested in "traits," the onlooker sees the object as an existent. This is still not the decisive mode of perception, which occurs when the man or thing encountered cannot be grasped objectively and yet "speaks" to the perceiver in a way that engages him in his whole being or life: "This man is not my object; I have got to do with him. . . . a word demanding an answer has happened to me." We may term this mode of perception *becoming aware*. And Buber continues:

> It by no means needs to be a man of whom I become aware. It can be an animal, a plant, a stone. No kind of appearance or event is fundamentally excluded from the series of the things through which from time to time something is said to me. Nothing can refuse to be the vessel for the Word. (10)

This brings us back to Williams' egalitarian poetics; it also, in the context of Buber's thought, indicates how a basically I-It relation can be elevated into an I-Thou one. "Nothing can refuse to be the vessel for the Word"; all things are potential partners in dialogue—whether they speak in paint, shape, sound, or, as does poetry, language itself.

In calling Jewish art "liturgical" (public and ethical) in contradistinction to avant-garde (experimental, "aesthetic," and appealing only to a coterie), Ozick was clearly in harmony with Buber's communal ideals, just as Buber criticizes the "radical aestheticizing of the relationship to things" (*Knowledge of Man,* 99). It is true that Buber was talking about the mescaline hallucinations of Aldous Huxley but his words on this subject are relevant to the whole question about what constitutes an "idolatrous" art or way of experiencing the world.

The radical aestheticizing of the relationship to things means here "penetrating and being received into the world of the senses." This drug-induced experience is called by Huxley "sacramental vision," a misnomer in that true sacrament involves the "participation, verified in life and death, of the whole person who has known the contact of the transcendent in his corporeal existence" (99). But the mescaline consumer, far from participating freely in a "common being," enters a "strictly private special sphere," a state of situationlessness that is in its essence uncommunal, while every situation, even the situation of those who [consciously] enter into solitude, is enclosed in the community of logos and cosmos" (100).

All the things of the world, the Hasids tell us, are filled with divine sparks; for men to embrace God's creation in all its corporeality is not sacrilege but sacrament. What is idolatry or sacrilege is wholly a matter of the human response to the object, and one man's idol may well be another's sacrament. In "radical aestheticism" we seek to escape from human reality (Ozick) or situation (Buber) by giving ourselves up to the sensations stimulated by the things around us, thereby cutting ourselves off from all others in a sterile and literally meaningless solitude. But the same things may address others in such a way that they respond with their "whole being" and are "confirmed in [their] selfhood" rather than sacrificing it for the situationless sensations offered by a false religion of art.

But all religions of art are false even though art of a certain kind is fundamental to religion. For Buber, man says Thou to God only embracing creation with his "whole" self. The Hungarian-Jewish art historian Ernest Namenyi, in his *Essence of Jewish Art (Esprit de l'art juife),* makes this

Art and Idolatry

very point in attempting to justify both the liturgical and aesthetic elements in art and poetry. He asks how man can know—say Thou to—an unknowable God unless He be approached through metaphor and image:

> The metaphors and imagery of synagogal poetry grant us access to the abstraction that is in the nature of our conception of God, and make it possible for us to grasp it. Only the emotion generated by liturgical poetry, prayer, and song could still endow the Absolute with an external form which the common people could understand; only this emotion can ensure an intimate communion between the ego of a man as he prays with God whom he addresses as Thou. (33)

On the other hand, only with the "aid of a powerful aesthetic impulse which seeks its fruition in song, in gestures, in the creations of the *plastic arts*" can the necessary "symbolical transformations" be attained.

My point is simply that it is not the case that Jewish art, for fear of idolatry, never gets beyond the stage of craft. But, as Namenyi makes clear in his discussion of the friezes at the Dura Europos temple in ancient Syria, it is an art that avoids idolatry by concentrating on events, not individual characters (or objects):

> The divine Will appeared, in continuous narrative, in concrete forms, clear and expressed in terms of space. Each form was therefore expressed in its full reality, while events followed on another in detached succession.... [allowing] a more truthful awareness of a vast shifting reality to reveal itself in art, beyond an exact depicting of the features of men or gods. (14)

Despite the abyss of time and space that separates them, there is a relationship between the aesthetic theory underlying the friezes and that of modernist poetry in that, like the former, the latter is concerned with an "open" form that will express a vast shifting reality—that it, too, in recounting the development or vicissitudes of the poetic mind in its struggle to acquire knowledge or ideal language, often takes the shape of a "continuous narrative" that declares it an art of becoming rather than one of being and fixity.

A major difference, of course, is that the Absolute, if it exists at all in modernist poetry, is much more obscure than that heaven of the Jews.[1] Only in T. S. Eliot is God not of the poet's own creation and even then he may be taken for a "bleeding eidolon."

Be that as it may, our chief interest is in the so-called Objectivists, or, better, the group of four Jewish-American poets who reluctantly went by that name. Can one be both a Jew and an Objectivist without being an "idolater"? Regarded from an orthodox point of view, Objectivism means "graven images" and appeal to the senses, albeit to the higher or aesthetic ones. Arguing from the same premises in *Moses and Monotheism,* Freud said that the transition from paganism to belief in a single, invisible God represented an increase in spirituality over the senses—in other words, of the abstract over the concrete and particular or the "objectively there." But to David Miller (*The New Polytheism*) just the opposite is true: he thinks that monotheism is out of touch with the dynamic nature of things and only polytheism, the new task of which will be to narrate the stories of the Gods in concrete images, can revive "an irrelevant doctrinal theology which has abstracted itself out of life by managing to kill God." Miller always speaks of monotheism and never Judaism; he never confronts actual Jewish thought or, more important, actual Jewish feeling, in which, whatever else he might be, God is no dead abstraction. Buber deals with this very problem in *Eclipse of God* by taking his point of departure from Spinoza's theory of God's infinite attributes and progressing to a resolution in which God is both inaccessible and unknowable and accessible as a partner-in-dialogue.

Art and Idolatry

Objectivism may not be polytheistic, but it is certainly pluralistic in that it eschews the single Whole for an atomized world in which things shine out in their individuality. This question is part of the larger one that emerges from the Jewish repudiation of aestheticism in general and before we deal with one we must try to resolve the other. Chaim Potok's novel *My Name Is Asher Lev* is one of the most vivid accounts we have of the antagonism between "Christian" or "Western" art and traditional Judaism, and the family strife in which it results. "Painting is for *goyim*," says Asher's mother. "Jews don't draw and paint." And that is the alpha and omega of the problem.

11 Asher Lev:
The Mariolatry of a Hasid

Born with a gift for painting, Chaim Potok's Asher Lev at an early age acquires a special kind of vision: "I could feel with my eyes," he tells us; "I felt myself flooded with the shapes and textures of the world around me" (*My Name Is Asher Lev*, 105–6). And contemplating the paintings of his mentor, Jacob Kahn, he speaks of their raw sensuousness moving against him. This awakening of an aesthetic consciousness or "objectivist" mode of perception confirms Asher's dedication to his art and introduces what will become the primary source of both joy and anguish in his life. To the horror of his mother (and, when he finds out, his father), Asher's genius leads him to the museum, where he copies Jesus and, eventually, nude women. "Do you know how much Jewish blood has been spilled because of him?" his mother asks. "How could you spend your precious time doing this?" (165).

Asher's reply makes no more sense to his mother than the deed itself: "I needed the expression, Mama. I couldn't find that expression anywhere else" (165). By concentrating on technique, Asher is pursuing a formalism that is wholly alien to the religious tradition out of which he comes, and it is finally his father, the very embodiment of this tradition, whom he must resist if he is to survive as an artist.

First, he is warned by his uncle that his principle obligation is to "read" Torah and that anything else is a waste of time. ("What kind of boy spends his whole life drawing? It kills the brain"—158). Even the part-time cook, Mrs. Rackover, takes up the theme: "What kind of a Jewish child was I? My father was giving his life for Torah . . . and I was wasting my life with paint. Goyim behaved this way toward their fathers, not Jews" (159).

Aryeh Lev, emissary of the leader (Rebbe) of the Hasidic Ladover sect, is currently engaged in a monumental effort to establish a network of Yeshivas, colleges for Scriptural studies, in the Soviet Union and Europe. When he learns about his son's aspirations and sees the kind of fruit they have been bearing, he experiences a rage equal to his stature. Rage will not, however, win back his son's soul.

Asher finds support in an art book given to him by his mother, who is vainly trying to reconcile father and son. Its credo is the perfect antithesis to Judaic beliefs:

> . . . every great artist is a man who has freed himself from his family, his nation, his race. Every man who has shown the world the way to beauty, to true culture, has been a rebel, a "universal" without patriotism, without home, who has found his people everywhere. (195)

Although this statement seems to be applicable to himself, Asher never uses it to justify his feelings, for he knows that it will only further antagonize Aryeh Lev, who would see the notion as coming from the "Other Side," a product of *goyische* reasoning, with its frivolous ideas about beauty and individualism. In the belief that his only hope lies in educating his father to the theory and technique of art, Asher launches into a series of technical explanations that brings more confusion than understanding, and ends in complete silence on both sides.

Although Potok has emphasized Asher's struggle to develop his talent in the face of all opposition, he has by no means made his main character into a single-minded rebel. Thus Asher repudiates neither family nor religion: the struggle with his father is actually based on love and, as I've just indicated, a desire to convince, not on the profound enmity inherent in the true Oedipal situation; accordingly, he continues to venerate the Rebbe and to follow Hasidic practices. Moreover, he is preoccupied with a distant ancestor, a Jew, he says, "who made a Russian nobleman rich by tending his estates." The nobleman turned out to be a "despotic goy," a "degenerate whose debaucheries grew wilder as he grew wealthier," and finally led to his murdering several serfs and burning down a village.

Since his ancestor had made the nobleman wealthy, Asher broods, wasn't he also partly responsible for the atrocities? Was it a sense of guilt that drove him to make the kind of journey that, repeated by his grandfather and father, represented an unknowing act of atonement carried out through the generations? And did he, Asher, interrupt that act by his "need to give meaning to paper and canvas rather than to people and events?" (309).

Asher transforms his anguish not into action but into a series of paintings—sixty of them—that depicts the life of his ancestor. True to his aesthetic vision, however, he sees these paintings chiefly in formal terms and nothing that he says about them conveys any idea of their ultimate meaning. All questions concerning the guilt of the generations and the need to atone for an ancient sin must go unanswered, just as must all questions about Asher's identity as a Hasid.[1]

Whatever the case, it is not these paintings that outrage Asher's parents and the Hasidic community and lead to his banishment by the Rebbe. It is *Brooklyn Crucifixion*, a study of his mother bound hand and foot in cruciform fashion to the living room window fixtures in the Lev apartment. Flanked by her husband, who holds a briefcase, and her son, who holds a palette, she reveals a lifetime of suffering and torment, the main one being that inflicted by the rival demands of father and son. Thus Asher sees himself as an "observant Jew working on a crucifixion because there was no aesthetic mold in his own religious tradition into which he could pour a painting of ultimate anguish and torment." He can say this in spite of the crucifixion's being anathema to his parents, as is *that man,* Christ, for having been responsible for the massacre of the Jews throughout history.

Obviously, more than aesthetic principle is involved here; Asher is flouting Jewish Law, not just the sensibilities of his mother and father, and he is doing so not just in being an artist but in compounding the transgression by treating his subject in the specific way he does. In copying Michelangelo's *Piéta,* Asher changes Christ into Mary, just as in the final version of the *Crucifixion* he changes Mary into his mother. This is a kind of Mariolatry, an apotheosis of the woman as the object of adoration and therefore the creation of a "false god."

Now, as Buber explains it, the mystical tradition, accepted by the Hasids, did in fact have, in the Shekina, a divine feminine principle associated with suffering and separation from God.[2] But as a principle it has never had the impact on Judaism that the Virgin had on Christianity and this failure is reflected in Asher's turning to the myths and symbols of the Enemy for inspiration. In other words, he is driven to Christianity as an outlet not only for his artistic talents but for his mother worship as well. With its view of art as a graven image and of the woman as a false object of worship, Judaism holds no hope for Asher. As one scholar put it, "due to the elimination of feminine images and symbols from day-to-day practices," Judaism became a "more barren, masculine repository of values."

The ironic truth, however, is that Asher is torn not between Christianity, as such, and Judaism, but between Judaism and paganism or primitivism. This dualism is expressed in Asher's very apparel, for he paints wearing a shirt and shorts with a tefillen wrapped about his arm; also described as emulating Jacob Kahn, who paints in the heat stripped to the waist, Asher seems to be very much the primitive painter, a quality confirmed by his masterpiece. *Brooklyn Crucifixion* fuses these elements—Christianity, Judaism, paganism, and primitivism—into a single vision. Compared to the sixty separate drawings in the mythic ancestor series, *Brooklyn Crucifixion II* is virtually as unified an apprehension as it is possible for Asher Lev to attain.

There is no little wisdom in the Rebbe's suggestion (command) that Asher remove himself from the Brooklyn Hasidic community and enroll in a Yeshiva in Paris. This is not an excommunication so much as the Rebbe's recognition that Asher, who must struggle to remain a Jew as much as to become an artist, suffers from his own form of psychological and spiritual schizophrenia. Faced with his first exhibition, he imagines warning his skeptical uncle, "You will see strange crucifixions painted by a Ladover Hasid who prays three times a day and believes in the Ribbono Shel Olam [Master of the Universe] and loves his parents and the Rebbe." We know that the strangest one of all, the as yet uncreated *Brooklyn Crucifixion III*, can only be a portrait of the artist himself.[3]

12 Reznikoff's Dispersion

Having summarily denied that there ever was such a thing as objectivism and claimed that the very choice of the name was arbitrary, Louis Zukofsky, Charles Reznikoff, Carl Rakosi, and George Oppen are still perceived by the world as the Objectivists. Indeed, when called upon to define the term as they understood it, each one of these writers indicated a certain, if general, relation to the others. Reznikoff, for instance, cites a Chinese text of the eleventh century in which it is argued that "Poetry presents the thing in order to convey the feeling. It should be precise about the thing and reticent about the feeling." This, Reznikoff tells us, was a very accurate expression of what the Objectivists were trying to do. Later, he elaborated on the term, at the same time describing the poetics of *Testimony,* a two-volume survey of the everyday cruelties of American life: by "objectivist I suppose a writer may be meant who does not write directly about his feelings but about what he sees and hears; who is restricted almost to the testimony of a witness in a court of law; and who expresses his feelings indirectly by the selection of his subject-matter" (Dembo and Pondrom, 206–9).

In his usual elliptical manner Zukofsky equates "objectification" (and "sincerity") with "thinking with the things as they exist." "I come into a room and I see a table. Obviously, I can't make it eat grass. I have delimited this thing, in a sense. I call it a table and I want to keep the word for the denotative sense—as solid as possible" (217). For Rakosi, the objectivist let his feelings depend upon the thing (about which he was writing) and was faithful to it; in contrast the symbolist was concerned with "a poetic state of feeling," which he sought to reproduce. "It really didn't matter what you started with—whether it was a flower or the moon" (201).

In Oppen's view the poet constructed "a method of thought . . . from the imagist intensity of vision . . . a 'test of truth' . . . anyway, a 'test of sincerity'—that there is a moment, an actual time, when you believe something to be true, and you construct a meaning from these moments of conviction" (174). Elsewhere he says, "I suppose it's nearly a sense of awe, simply to feel that the thing is there and that it's quite something to see. It's an awareness of the world, a lyric reaction to the world" (177).

Now, of this group, Reznikoff is perhaps the most accessible. His poetry has none of the impenetrability of Zukofsky's or Oppen's or even the moderate obscurity of Rakosi's; indeed it is this very "simplicity" of language and philosophy that has thrown him into sharp relief from the others. This is not to say that Reznikoff isn't an Objectivist, for if Zukofsky was the "philosophical" leader of the group (and I'm not at all sure Oppen would have consented to this), then it was the poetry of Reznikoff that had the most appeal for the others. Zukofsky, himself, it will be recalled, gave over a large part of his now-famous article on "sincerity" and "objectification" to poems by Reznikoff in which these central characteristics were perceived. And questioned as to whether he felt that his work was closest to Williams Carlos Williams', Rakosi replied, "Well, no. I would say the one who is closest to me is Charles Reznikoff . . . [He] comes through in his earlier poems as a thoroughly compassionate man. He comes through as a person.

When he's observing something, you're inside him" (203). But the most illuminating response comes from Oppen, who paid Reznikoff this tribute in a foreword to the second volume of the collected poems:

> the girder, still itself
> among the rubble
>
> > That line of Reznikoff's and the poem of which it is a part, and line upon line of his perfect poems have been with me for the forty-eight years since I first came upon them. If we had no other poetry I think we could nevertheless live by virtue of these poems, these lives, these small precise, these overwhelming gentle iron lines and images of all that it is and our love and pride and small life which is immeasurable as these lines which are still themselves among the rubble. (*Complete Poems*, 2:7)

This statement is Oppen's complete foreword. Wholly typical of his way of looking at poetry and life, it says all that need be said of a man who possesses, as Oppen called it elsewhere, that "virtue of the mind . . . that emotion which causes to see" (186). To repeat Oppen's definition of objectivism cited above, this virtue is the ability "to feel that the thing is there and that it's quite something to see" (186). Providing the images for poetry, these things are part of the facts and details of "our small life"—small in one sense, immeasurable in another.

Ironically, the poetic principle implied here has been associated with that of the writer whose role in the origin and development of objectivism has, according to all involved, been greatly overestimated: namely, William Carlos Williams. Thus what Oppen means when he says that "the most tremendous and compelling emotion we possess is the one that forces us to look, to know, to *see*" is almost the same thing Williams does when he speaks of "seeing the thing itself without forethought or afterthought but with great intensity of perception." The true value, Williams tells us, "is that peculiarity which gives an object a character by itself. The associational or sentimental value is the false." What stands in the way of good writing, he adds, is "the virtual impossibility of lifting to the imagination those things which lie under the direct scrutiny of the senses, under the nose"—in other words, the "small" facts and details of everyday life (*Selected Essays*, 5, 11).

What this comes down to, partly, in Oppen, Williams, and Reznikoff (as well as in Zukofsky and Rakosi) is the attempt to discover the beautiful in mean objects, usually in an industrial or urban setting.[1] "January Morning" is an anatomy of aesthetic values in Williams' world:

> —and the sun, dipping into the avenues
> streaking the tops of
> the irregular houselets,
>   and
> the gay shadows dropping and dropping.
> . . . .
> —and a young horse with a green bed-quilt
> on his withers shaking his head:
> bared teeth and nozzle high in the air!
> . . . .
> —and the worn,
> blue car rails (like the sky!)
> gleaming among the cobbles!
>   (*Collected Early Poems*, 162–66)

Jerusalem the Golden (1934) records Reznikoff's lyric response to the same world:

> This smoky winter morning—
> do not despise the green jewel among the twigs
> because it is a traffic light.

> A black horse and a white horse, pulling a truck this winter day,
> as the smoke of their nostrils reaches to the ground,
> seem fabulous.

Reznikoff's Dispersion

And here is the original of the lines that stayed with Oppen for a lifetime:

> Among the heaps of brick and plaster lies
> a girder, still itself among the rubbish.
>
> (1:116, 117, 121)

For Oppen the girder is a "lyric valuable," one of those objects that causes us "to see"; it is also, explicitly, lines of poetry and, by inference, the poet himself. For Reznikoff it was that and perhaps something more.

If all four Objectivists were Jewish, only Reznikoff is centrally concerned with Judaism: the biblical history of Israel, the Jewish immigrant experience in America (his own as a second generation American and that of his family), and the Holocaust. "A girder, still itself among the rubbish/rubble" is the very image to describe the Jews and their long story of survival amid devastation by their enemies. "From the rubbish heaps that are Jerusalem / rebuild the city; replant the land." Thus invokes a speaker in the Babylonian vignette of *In Memoriam*. As the whole section makes clear, the critical problem of Jewish survival in the Diaspora is not always physical but often cultural, and involves not existence but identity.

It is the appeal of Babylonian civilization that threatens the exile; here the "girder" is more than a "lyric valuable"; it is an ethical one as well:

> but we must build in Babylon
>   another Zion
> of precepts, laws, ordinances and commandments
> to outlast stone or metal,
> between every Jew and the fury or blandishment of any
> land.
>
> (1:141)

A shield against anti-Semitism (fury) and foreign spiritual and physical temptations, the Scriptures are the basis of

3. False Gods, Graven Images

the homogeneity and unity of Jewish communal life and its perpetuation.

Given an American education but not a Jewish one, Reznikoff feels himself to be without such protection:

> in spite of all the learning I had acquired in high school,
> I knew not a word of the sacred text of the Torah
> and was going out into the world
> with none of the accumulated wisdom of my people to guide me,
> with no prayers with which to talk to the God of my people, a soul—
> for it is not easy to be a Jew or, perhaps, a man—
> doomed by his ignorance to stumble and blunder.
> (2:167)

Nevertheless, we find him apologizing for America after his grandfather had been bullied by anti-Semites:

> [He] tried to explain that what had happened was unusual,
> that only the neighborhood we lived in was like that, and
> what a wonderful country this was—
> that all our love for it and our praise
> was not unmerited. (2:155)

But there is more to it. Reznikoff was dogged by anti-Semitism throughout his childhood. Indeed, his life as a loner and wanderer, no less than much of his irony and wit, has its source in fears and anxieties elicited by Jew-baiting youths. Still, even these experiences were not enough to embitter him; he learned to adapt himself:

> Scorn
> shall be your meat
> instead of praise;
> you shall eat and eat of it
> all your days,
> and grow strong on it
> and live long on it, Jew.
> (2:22)

Anti-Semitism was always on, or in the back of, his mind:

> On a seat in the subway, staring out of the window at
> the noisy darkness, why are you sad?
> You are not a Hebrew:
> you would have no trouble getting a job.
> (2:23)

But this was America, not Russia with its pogroms or Germany with its death camps. Anti-Semitism is not state policy and the poet's response, wit and irony, is still appropriate.

As both poet and man, Reznikoff finds himself torn between his identity as an American and as a Jew. When the Jew in him speaks, he feels the inadequacy of the life lived as an individual, "privately as an animal," and makes resolutions:

> I have eaten whatever I liked,
> I have slept as long as I wished,
> I have left the highway like a dog
> to run into every alley;
> Now I must learn to fast and watch....
> I will fast for you, Judah,
> and be silent for you
> and wake in the night because of you;
> I will speak for you
> in psalms,
> and feast because of you
> on unleavened bread and herbs.
> (2:25–26)

This poem is part of a sequence called "A Short History of Israel, Notes and Glosses" and the poet speaks as though he were part of that history. His notion of sin and penitence, his desire to return to the fold—all indicate that the claims of the Diaspora upon him are weakening. But this

3. False Gods, Graven Images

is only one side of the issue. Another sequence, significantly called "Autobiography: New York," celebrates not the communal values of Jewish tradition, but those of the lone man in a world of lyric valuables:

> I like the sound of the street—
> but I, apart and alone,
> beside an open window
> and behind a closed door.
> (2:27)

This is indeed a different world, a different context, from that of the Old Testament. There are no righteous Israelites or their jealous God to scrutinize the speaker, who, himself is no David dancing before the Lord, but only an unimportant, nameless, monological denizen of the city.

Without a Jewish education, Reznikoff finds that the effort to become a Jew is too onerous. His studies seem only to increase his awareness of separation:

> How difficult for me is Hebrew:
> even the Hebrew for *mother*, for *bread*, for *sun* is foreign.
> How far I've been exiled, Zion.
> (1:72)

Unfortunately, as the little poem that Zukofsky admired for its sound patterns tells us, the language of the *goyim* is none too easy, either:

> As I, barbarian, at last, although slowly, could read Greek, at "blue-eyed Athena"
> I greeted her picture that had long been on the wall: the head slightly bent forward under the heavy helmet, as if to listen, the beautiful lips slightly scornful.
> (1:107)

Addressing what appears to be no more than a faded picture, the poet, in his imagination, has brought Athena to life—despite "Thou shalt not worship graven images" and "Thou shalt have no other Gods before me." She appears to him exactly the way a civilized deity would appear to a barbarian or a Jew in exile. Her head bends forward under the weight of the helmet, but the poet imagines himself to be speaking too low and too hesitantly to be heard and he thinks he sees in her face nothing but scorn, both for his bad Greek and because he is a Jew. False God, graven image, *shikse,* Athena, Goddess of Western Wisdom, is the very epitome of blandishment and menace to young romantic Jews. Athena is bad enough; "worship" of the moon (or, implicitly, Artemis) can bring utter disaster:

> The moon shines in the summer night;
> now I begin to understand the Hebrews
> Who could forget the Lord, throw kisses at the moon,
> until the archers came against Israel
> and bronze chariots from the north
> rolled into the cities of Judah and the streets of Jerusalem.
> (1:107)

For throwing kisses at the moon the Hebrews are severely punished by a jealous God. What must his own punishment be, wonders the poet, for looking not only at the moon but at "stars and trees" as well. Only the prophets can say.

The sin of throwing kisses at the moon is that of lust ("Shameless moon, naked upon a cloudless sky / Showing your rose and silvery bosom / to all the city"), but it is the kind of lust that only a poet would experience. It is also the sin of loving nature above God, of going one's Separate Way, of fighting "the enemies" of my people with the fanciful weapons that only a poet would forge:

> I will write songs against you
> ... I will pelt you
> with the winged seeds of the dandelion;
> I will marshal against you
> the fireflies of the dusk.
> (1:168)

3. False Gods, Graven Images

True the poet fights with weapons that only he is capable of using but are they really enough to daunt the enemies of Zion? Can the anti-Semite be conquered by song, dandelion seeds, and fireflies? Not in Judah, certainly; and not even in civilized Babylon.

On the streets of New York, Reznikoff perceives lyric valuables and radiant natural objects everywhere. Yet he is too skeptical to miss the ugliness and malevolence that are equally ubiquitous. Not that any of the poems have an explicit moral theme; indirect expression of feelings is the basic principle that Reznikoff lends to and draws from objectivism and he can be wholly opaque to those too eager to find a didactic purpose in his lyrics. On the other hand, a little speculation sometimes reveals an otherwise invisible dimension of meaning. What, if anything, should be made of this, for example:

> this stout gentleman,
> who needs a shave badly,
> leaning in an arbor hung with purple grapes,
> purple grapes all about him,
> is unpleasant.
> Am I becoming misanthropic?
> An atheist?
> Why this might be the god Bacchus!
> (2:32)

The poet reproaches himself for his aversion to an unkempt fat man in a grape arbor. Terms like misanthropic and atheist might misleadingly suggest that an authentic moral or religious question were being raised, but the concluding line makes the whole episode the material of wit. If the poet fears that he is an atheist, it is from the pagan not the Hebraic point of view. That is, he is saying, "Were I a true believer, I'd have known at once that I might be in the presence of Bacchus." This is indeed a long way from

Zion. It is also, as a matter of fact, a long way from New York. Who, in Manhattan, believes in Bacchus, anyway? Only pagan poets and dispersed Jews? Or perhaps nobody but Reznikoff, himself.

And the Greek gods do appear to him on his sojourns through the city. We have seen him in his lack of personal importance choose freedom, but none of the secular joys and delights of Babylon can bring him true ease or satisfaction. He sums up the experience of the cultured Jew, himself in particular, in this warning:

> You understand the myths of the Aztecs
> and read with sympathy
> the legends of the Christian saints
> and say proudly:
> though you were born a Jew
> there is nothing Jewish about you.
> But the ancient Greeks would still have thought you a barbarian
> and even the Christian saints might not have liked you;
> and the Nazis
> would have pried from your witty mouth
> your golden teeth.
> (2:103)

But, as I've said before, it is not only anti-Semitism that makes Reznikoff sit down by the waters of Babylon to weep. Here is the sequel, quoted in its entirety, to a poem discussed earlier:

> Give me the strength
> To dance before your ark
> as King David did.
> (2:105)

Strength here means the strength to acquire a discipline that will confirm the poet in the ways (rituals) of his ancestors.

3. False Gods, Graven Images

In this state of mind, Reznikoff ceases to be the Objectivist or observer of lyric valuables and becomes, in effect, prophet, psalmist, bard:

> Out of the strong, sweetness;
> and out of the dead body of the lion of Judah,
> the prophecies and the psalms;
>   out of the slaves in Egypt,
>   out of the wandering tribesmen of the deserts
>   and the peasants of Palestine,
>   out of the slaves of Babylon and Rome,
>   out of the ghettoes of Spain and Portugal, Germany and Poland
>   the Torah and the prophecies,
>   the Talmud and the sacred studies, the hymns and songs of the Jews.
> (2:61)

Among the most powerful in Reznikoff's poetry, these lines are part of the Lord's Song, even though, paradoxically, they are rendered in a Whitmanian American-English (Babylonian, in other words). Nevertheless, can't it be said that, after all, the poem is written in Reznikoff's native tongue and that Whitman, like all poets, speaks for all mankind—so that if a Hebrew prophet were to speak in English to a twentieth-century audience, he would speak like Whitman/Reznikoff?

But Judaism, like its God, is not given to compromise and the poet will simply have to learn Hebrew. Otherwise, he might just as well have studied Greek, devoted himself to Athena, and worshipped (along with Ezra Pound) the lyric valuables that held her name. It's hard to see Reznikoff as a prophet or even as a psalmist: he seems too compassionate for that even in his ironic poems. But even he was thinking of schism, not compromise, when he said:

> The tendency is, on the one hand, to be assimilated and, on the other, to be yourself. Some people accentuate one or

the other, but assimilation has historically been common among Jews. It's in one's nature to become part of the surrounding community. (Dembo and Pondrom, 212)

Being himself, however, really meant not just a Jew or just an American but both and neither. When he wrote Objectivist poems, he was an Objectivist; when he wrote of "his people" he was, in a manner of speaking, a psalmist. He is by turns Israelite, Babylonian, New Yorker—would-be journalist, nonpracticing lawyer, city-walker. An exile, he sits down by the waters of Manhattan to weep; a wry smile comes over his face, for he realizes that he is home. And then he really weeps.

13 The Objectivist Jew

The problem of the Jew in the Diaspora as expressed by Reznikoff is implicit in the poetry of Zukofsky and Oppen even though Judaism appears to be only peripheral in Zukofsky and scarcely even that in Oppen. Having spent almost a decade in Mexico, where he fled during the McCarthy epoch, Oppen had a full knowledge of what living in exile meant; and one of the evils was the absence of a readership for his poetry and of a current language in which to write at all. Zukofsky it is true never left New York but, having lived his life as a recluse, was a self-exile. Despite his being born and raised in orthodoxy by immigrant parents, Zukofsky, in his poetry, indicates a break with both Jewish tradition and American culture. "Assimilation is not hard," says Zukofsky in "Poem Beginning 'The,' " a highly fragmented work that seems to be a parody of *The Waste Land*. "And once the Faith's askew / I might as well look Shagetz [gentile] just as much as Jew." But neither can Zukofsky identify himself with middle-class America, and we find him quoting Yehoash (Samuel Bloomgarden, the Yiddish writer) who provides what is clearly a metaphor for the condition of the non-Jewish Jewish poet in America:

> And his heart is dry
> Like teeth of dead camel

> But his eyes no longer blink
> Not even as a blind dog's.
> With the blue night shadows on the sand
> May his kingdom return to him,
> The Bedouin leap again in his *asilah,*
> The expanse of heaven hang upon his shoulder. . . .[1]

The trouble is that the poet, cut off from his traditions, has neither language nor voice to sing the Lord's Song in an alien land; unlike Yehoash he can make only "kleinen lieder," not "great songs" based on religious faith.

This situation explains a good deal about Zukofsky's notorious obscurity and is directly relevant to Oppen's. Recording an exchange between Louis and her husband, Mary Oppen gives us an insight into the possible dimensions of this issue. Zukofsky has asked George an unanswerable question that George answers immediately: "Do you like your own poetry better than mine?" "Yes." "George," Mary continues, "insisting on clarity and understanding, speaking of his difficulty in knowing if the readers would understand; Louis, with a shrug replying, 'It doesn't matter, they don't care if they understand you or not.' . . . Not knowing how to say it without insulting Louis, but implying that Louis used incomprehensibility as a tactic, George said, 'You're tougher than I am, Louis,' referring to Louis' disregard of the reader."[2]

To anyone who has looked into Oppen's first collection, *Discrete Series* (1930), to say nothing of later work like *Seascape: Needle's Eye* (1972) or *Primitive* (1979), Oppen and Zukofsky are pot and kettle when it comes to incomprehensibility. Yet neither of them is obscure for frivolous reasons. "I have not and never did have any motive of poetry / But to achieve clarity," says Oppen in "Route," and indeed his cry for "the most beautiful thing in the world, / A limited, limiting clarity" (*Collected Poems,* 185) arises from the core of his emotional life. There is, in other words, a dialogical dimension to his view both of himself as an actual person and as a poetic persona.

3. False Gods, Graven Images

Ideally, the "public utterance" that is the poem "reports" an actuality or a truth experienced, felt, or perceived by the poet. More often, however, such utterance is nothing more than "the ferocious mumbling, in public / Of rootless speech" (159). This is so because in Oppen's existential world only the individual man can determine what is meaningful and valuable in his own life, and he is beset by confusion and doubt, forced by the conditions of existence to be a monologist and all the while seeking to "rescue / Love to the ice-lit / Upper World a substantial language / Of clarity and of respect" ("Narrative" in *Collected Poems*, 140). "I stumble over these stories," Oppen writes, "Progeny, the possibility of progeny, continuity, / or love that tempted him / He is punished by place, by scene, by all that holds all he has found" (139). Place and scene are the "materials" of reality or truth; they punish the poet because they stubbornly remain matter rather than allowing themselves to be rendered into form, an act that is Oppen's aesthetic approximation of Buber's dialogical event:

> this pavement, the silent symbols
> Of it, the word of it, never more powerful than in this moment. Well, hardly an epiphany, but there the thing is all the same
> (193)

It is precisely the finite in its limited, limiting clarity that Oppen seeks, but "infiniteness is the most evident thing in the world" (174) and the poet cannot find his bearings:

> We want to defend
> Limitation
> And do not know how. . . .
> And cannot defend
> The metaphysic
> On which rest
> The boundaries
> Of our differences
> (165)

In one sense, Oppen's view of the world is thoroughly grounded in materialism; he seeks the finite in all its clarity and sharpness of definition. Reality becomes truth when it reifies itself, registers upon the poetic sensibility, and the poet feels its presence. The "lyric valuable" by which he expresses his experience may not be an "idol," but it is a "graven image" having no existence or meaning beyond the poet's "sensual" awareness of it.

In his study of Hasidic thought, Buber did say that man must grasp the creator through his creation. Yet this is exactly the problem for Oppen in whose world there is no divinity to whom things can be consecrated, no God to establish a unity out of the infinite number of meanings that things, which "explain each other, not themselves," pour forth. Oppen's desire to discover whether the "numerosity" of human beings constitutes a unity called "humanity," whether the seascape is more than the "needle's eye" of waves, whether the "thousand threads in his hands" can be woven into one whole fabric are all expressions of his lifelong attempt to attain the certain knowledge in which finitude is joined to purpose in a nonteleological universe and the obscurities of the material world as well as those of symbols that have no connection with a lived, worldly reality are dispelled.

Obscurity, then, is as inevitable a part of Oppen's poetry as it is of his life—indeed, paradoxically, it is part of the "meaning" in both. The illumination that brings definition and certitude eludes the poet, and the poem is "messed" (Oppen's word). Thus Oppen, whose social consciousness led him in the thirties to abandon poetry and join the Communist party, ironically becomes, when he begins writing again after twenty-five years, not a social realist but a Kierkegaardian existentialist, and not a reader of Torah in dialogue with man and God but a monologist—not by choice or whim, that is certain, but because integrity or "sincerity" to one's self, along with a resistant reality and an even more resistant language, made him so.

3. False Gods, Graven Images

This characterization is borne out by Oppen's interviews, and not just by his willingness to be interviewed in the first place or in his obvious pleasure in exchanging ideas with a sympathetic reader. He reveals here that whatever the nature of his mental, material, or metaphysical worlds, he is in essence no solipsist and no willing monologist: "I have, just on a human basis, a kind of liking for openness and a willingness to talk and question; and if one says something that is wrong, so one says something that is wrong." And he adds that poetry was meant to

> bridge certain gaps between temperament to reach common ground, in spite of differences in temperament. After all, it's one of the very crucial and difficult questions of . . . poetry, whether within these differences in one's personal vision . . . one can reach common ground. One always finds that one can—that's the very wonderful thing. (*George Oppen: Man and Poet*, 212)

If Mary Oppen is correct in saying that George was implicitly accusing Zukofsky of using incomprehensibility and obscurity as a "tactic," we might well wonder just what "tactic" means in this context. If it means that Zukofsky was maliciously and deliberately obscure because he was contemptuous, we must disagree; but if it means that, deliberate or not, obscurity was part of the structure and substance of his poetry, we applaud the insight. We have already seen that Zukofsky was, as a poet, engaged in a struggle for articulation (or communication) under conditions psychologically and philosophically similar to those that concerned Oppen. And like the interview with Oppen, that with Zukofsky has much to tell us on this issue, although in a very different way.

In his study of Zukofsky's "*A*," Barry Ahearn took exception to my line of questioning. He was put off by the impression that I had had to persuade Zukofsky to sit for the interview in the first place since he was "not comforta-

The Objectivist Jew

ble in interviews, and eventually . . . avoided them altogether." That may be so, but in this particular interview Zukofsky was in no way perturbed by anything that was said. Far from it, he spoke with complete self-assurance. The passage in question concerns the imagery in one of the early poems (see *All*, 24):

> Q. Where do the leopard and the dragon fit in?
> A. That's the constellation. "Leopard, glowing-spotted, / The summer river— / Under."
> Q. Why do you refer to the constellation?
> A. There I'm . . . not for metaphor unless, as Aristotle says, you bring together unlikes that have never existed before. But they're in words; they're in verbs: "the sun rises." My statements are often very, very clipped.
> Q. Well, the colon in the last line after "Under" would seem to imply that the dragon is under the river.
> A. "Summer river—/Under: . . ." There is a question of movement and enough rest; notice the space after "Under." The dragon is also reflected in the river—inverted.

It is Ahearn's opinion that this exchange "floundered in a bog of cross-purposes." This is correct—moreover, it seems to have been true of the whole interview; the more voluble he became, the less Zukofsky could be understood. And it is not that he was trying to be obscure; quite the contrary, he thought he was being simple and clear and he remained serene and imperturbable throughout the whole discourse.

This episode, I daresay, is a reflection of Zukofsky's "continuous narrative," his unending struggle to transfigure into aesthetic form by the use of a language molded to the purpose the recalcitrant materials of his private, family, and social life. Conversely, no one was surprised to find Zukofsky maintaining that he wouldn't (or couldn't?) talk about the details of his private life even during those moments when, during informal conversation, he seemed to be doing that very thing.

3. False Gods, Graven Images

The whole question of obscurity can be seen as part of the larger question of the failed quest for an ideal poetic language, wherein it becomes the major theme of a continuous narrative that insofar as it says what the author wanted it to say is, in fact, a successful poem. Here, the persona's failure is the poet's achievement. It can also be interpreted as being a literal failure, one in which the actual poet sought clarity but could not attain it. In the Buberian context, obscurity goes hand in glove with radical aestheticism; in the pursuit of beauty, sensation, form, language—all for its own sake—the poet must necessarily be a monologist, willingly or not. He is so because his "faith is askew" and he might as well be *shagetz* as Jew, Jew being defined here as someone who seeks relationship, dialogue, with others and not aesthetic sensation, individual apprehension or personal performance—assuming that the two are in fact incompatible.

But this may be assuming too much. Burton Hatlen has argued—and not implausibly—that the four Objectivist poets "felt a need to act in history and to take responsibility for other people," that being "secularized Jews," "they sought in Marxism a kind of 'universal Judaism,' which would allow all humankind to assume a conscious responsibility for making its own history." Thus, says Hatlen, they joined a Marxist politics to a Poundian poetics.[3]

Hatlen seems to be touching upon several issues here: the relation of Marxism to Judaism; the relation of Marxism and Judaism to aestheticism; the relation of Objectivist theories of language and history first to Judaism and then to the poetics of Ezra Pound; and finally the relation of Pound's fascism to Marxism. In these relationships Hatlen is seeking the very compatibility that I have taken to be absent. Despite the appeal of Marxism to "secularized Jews," to call it "a kind of universal Judaism" is to ignore not only the vast philosophic and ethical differences that separate them but the mutual exclusiveness of each and the assumption by each that it is complete in itself. It is true that both are socially oriented and on this point are distinguishable from aestheticism, a form of individualism, but their common abhorrence of "pagan" art or "bourgeois" art and its theories doesn't make them sympathetic to one another.

Whatever the case, it is misleading to say that the Objectivists joined a "Marxist politics with a Poundian poetics." Quite the contrary, two of them stopped writing altogether—Oppen, when he joined the Communist party; and Rakosi, when he went to work for a Jewish welfare agency. When Oppen put pen to paper again, it was, as I have noted, as an existentialist, not as a socialist. As for Zukofsky, Marxism plays a very small role in his work (Hatlen's absorbing essay on "A-8" notwithstanding); indeed, when classifying the poets under Pound's old rubrics, Hatlen himself sees Zukofsky—and rightly so—as being predominantly "melopoeic" (musical), not "logopoeic" (thematic) or "phanopoeic" (imagistic).

According to Hatlen, the Objectivists came to Pound's ideas about language and history by way of a "Jewish sense of speech as a sacred event, of language as, not 'about,' the world, but constitutive of it." And he believes that this way of thinking can be found in Martin Buber, who has reminded us of the ways in which "Judaism continues to be centered upon the act of address: God speaking to humankind, men and women speaking both to God and to one another, the solitary person speaking to a tree or a wall—speaking them into being." Thus he concludes that the Objectivists all found in Pound's " 'process poetics' . . . a similar sense of language as an on-going sacred event." "Similar," perhaps; but where does this leave us?

I suspect that the Objectivists did not reach Pound by way of the Jewish sense of language or history but accepted his "open" poetics directly and without much thought to either Pound's similarity to Buber, on the one hand, or his anti-Semitism, on the other. That is, their reasons for acknowledging Pound as an influence were wholly literary.

3. False Gods, Graven Images

Had they written as observant Jews or even "secular" Jews with a Buberian sense of language as a sacrament, they could not have been the "formalists" that they in fact are. They would in some way have carried the message of the Torah—for isn't that the definitive difference between the Scriptures (or literal sacrament and Logos) and man-made poetry that presumes to be Logos but can be so only by metaphor, since it is based not upon dialogue with God but upon the lyric song (or "lyric valuable") of the poet at the center of his own creation? In their continuous narratives the Objectivists are still writing in monologue or soliloquy; and is this not what some might call "aesthetic idolatry," in which the final idol is the self and the Logos obscurity?

Part Four
Anti-Semitism and the Monological Gentile

14 Pedagogy and/or Pedagoguery
Pound's Way

Martin Buber has written that there are two basic ways of influencing men in their views and attitudes toward life. In the first, he tells us,

> a man tries to impose himself, his opinion and his attitude, on the other in such a way that the latter feels the psychical result of the action to be his own insight, which has only been freed by the influence.

In the second, he continues,

> a man wishes to find and to further in the soul of the other the disposition toward what he has recognized in himself as the right. Because it is the right, it must also be alive in the microcosm of the other, as one possibility. The other need only be opened out in this potentiality of his; moreover, this opening out takes place not essentially by teaching, but by meeting, by existential communication between someone that is in actual being and someone that is in a process of becoming. (*Knowledge of Man*, 82)

The first way, Buber explains, is that of the propagandist; the second, that of the educator. This dichotomy can give us an insight into that most dichotomous of poets, Ezra Pound.

Pound, of course, saw himself as a unity; we see him as a bundle of contradictions. In one sense, Pound is justified—the sheer volume of books that offer to reveal the organizing principles of *The Cantos,* his "endlessly accreting" lifetime work, implies that Pound exhibited in his poetic life, and in his life in general, a "directio-voluntatis" that was an ideal of thought and action and possessed only by such great men as Jefferson and/or Mussolini. His poetics, which have been so influential that, rightly or wrongly, a whole era now bears his name, are seemingly based on the unwobbling pivot of the aesthetics of the Chinese character and the ethics of Confucius.

Now, there are no unresolved paradoxes in the Chinese view of the cosmos, calligraphy, or the human spirit. The well-known passage from the *Ta Hsueh* concerning the interrelationship of all things descending from heaven to the heart and ascending back to heaven bespeaks a natural and harmonious unity out of the great dualism represented by the Yin and the Yang.[1] But the dualisms we find in Pound's thought are not so tractable, even though we are led to believe that the Confucian model and its Western analogies are at the essence of his work. Pound's view of unity is attained only at heavy cost—not by *cheng ming,* the Confucian "rectification of terms" or verbal clarity by which things can be distinguished from one another, but rather by distinctions muddled in the service of an overall self image. One of the primary distinctions is that between the educator and the propagandist.

The instinct to teach not only was strong in Pound but dominated his whole personality; that much is evidenced by his correspondence, his family relations, his essays, his poetry—by, in fact, nearly everything he said or did. One biographer, E. Fuller Torrey, argues that far from suffering during his incarceration at St. Elizabeth's, Pound actually found life quite acceptable—in large part because he was

Pedagogy and/or Pedagoguery

allowed to "hold court" with his many visitors. But it is in the reason for his being at St. Elizabeth's in the first place, the broadcasts from Radio Rome made during the war, that the "teaching instinct," fueled by a compulsion to save the world, turned into a kind of megalomania in which the distinction between education and propaganda was wholly lost.

For Buber, education is one aspect of the I-Thou relationship, in which man meets man, not as the self encounters the Other in a competitive and an exploitive I-It situation, but in the mutual awareness of actual feelings and thought. The "meeting" is intensely human, intensely humanistic, presupposing as it does an intimacy on the highest plane.[2] In propaganda, on the other hand, there is no interplay, no exchange; indeed from the way Buber describes it, it seems that the recipient not only must accept all that is directed to him, but is duped into believing that the ideas are his own and are merely being released in him by the propagandist. In effect, propaganda is based on a form of dehumanization, of its recipient no less than its subject; as a weapon in warfare it could hardly be expected to be otherwise.

On the other hand, this is one case in which sincerity is even worse than cynical detachment. We can be sure that Pound believed what he said and indeed it was his total faith in his subject matter that caused him to conflate education and propaganda, to begin with. Furthermore, Pound never judged the propaganda form to be demeaning to his intelligence; verbal abuse is not absent in the *Cantos* nor is it alien to the translation of the Confucian odes. In these texts there is a diversity of targets and the reader, fortified by the lyrical passages, can withstand the shock of crass denunciation, especially when it is uttered by a persona. But in the radio speeches we receive the full measure of Pound's truly Manichean view of the world, a Kimmeria in which armies wage bloody battle while behind them international Jewry prepares for its economic and political assumption of global power. The duped peoples of Britain and America, shedding their blood for kikery, can be saved only by heeding the words of the Man Who Knows. Pound emerges as anti-Messiah and his Word is the anti-Logos.

But it is the anti-Word of a poet and historian of culture who knows what the true "Logos" can be, what it means, in short, to be a "Master of Utterance" and not just a wordsman. Both Daniel Perlman and Torrey (and, I'm sure, the majority of Pound scholars) have asked how a man of Pound's erudition, reverence for culture, and intellectual caliber in general could accept the notorious *Protocols of the Elders of Zion* as the basis for his anti-Semitism.

Pound's mode of thought, Perlman conjectures, is a kind of intuitionism in which traditional, plodding thought, the way of the discursive scholar, is held in contempt; "although it served him extremely well as imagist/vorticist poet," this anti-intellectual intuitionism "helps explain in part his gullibility to fascist propaganda." But does it? Are all intuitionists potential fascists awaiting only the appearance of an anti-Semitic myth to inspire them? Is the intuitionism that served Pound as an imagist the same as the one that led him to fascism? If so, what about H. D. or F. S. Flint, whose imagism did not make them anti-Semites?

Whether as an explanation or an excuse, this argument has had a certain attraction for Pound scholars. Even Torrey, clearly no sympathizer, tells us of Pound's belief that the "unusual man, the great artist, inevitably aims straight for the truth without such obstructions as human reasoning" (Torrey, 139). As Pound himself had put it in *Guide to Kulchur*, "By genius I mean an inevitable swiftness and rightness in a given field. . . . 'Human Greatness' is an unusual energy coupled with straightness, the direct shooting mind" (104–5; Torrey, 140). Torrey, of course, is not saying that he himself believes this argument to be valid; he is merely presenting it as a possible explanation as to how Pound could hold fascist or anti-Semitic views.

But even this apparent objectivity has biased implications

insofar as it suggests that if anti-Semitism is the product of a special form of knowledge, then all anti-Semites are geniuses or mystics. Torrey does say that Pound's "antipathy toward Jews became much more sophisticated and focused after he had been exposed to the teachings of the 'elders' of Zion." I'm not sure "sophisticated" is the right word here, but let that pass. The notion that any form of anti-Semitism, the natural expression of which is the language of propaganda, can be posited as a kind of superior knowledge makes a mockery not only of reason but of mystical thought as well. But Torrey doesn't help matters when, still seeking explanations, he asserts that "Pound's education was almost exclusively in languages and literature, not in history, economics, or the natural sciences." So much for a humanistic education as a shield against noxious doctrines.

The waters become even more muddied when Torrey introduces other opinions about why Pound believed the *Protocols* to be authentic. He cites with apparent approval, for instance, John Gwyer's view that "there has always been a belief that certain groups were conspiring to rule the world. . . . After a while one sees how convenient it really is. It saves so much thinking to think like this. . . . It has a fatal appeal to those who see the world as hostile and rejecting; it beckons as the Sirens once called to Odysseus" (Torrey, 142). This is, of course, not the problem at all. Since when has Pound been known to believe in anything because he was mentally lazy or it was "convenient"?

Besides, the *Protocols* were not written for the intellectually lazy; its language is that of the political tract and in the interests of giving his text credibility, the forger concedes to his putative Jewish authors a seeming rigor of argument. That is, if the *Protocols* were to be accepted as a revelation of the "Jewish Peril," the actual author not only required a knowledge of social and political institutions, but he had to forsake the usual caricature of supposedly Jewish traits. On at least one of these points he failed—

badly. The document, for all its apparent knowledge of politics and the social system, is, when it comes to Jewish affairs, permeated with oversimplifications, distortions of fact, and other travesties of argumentation. The author could replace loss of stereotype only with total ignorance of Jewish history, thought, and law. The very idea of achieving world domination, especially by the Machiavellian methods here presented, runs counter to the Jewish belief in a spiritual redemption that marks the coming of a Messiah. In fact, in his Hobbesian view of man, his desire for power, and his nihilism, the putative author cannot credibly speak for Jews at all; if he speaks for anyone, it is for the fascists themselves.

No, we pursue the final explanation for Pound's anti-Semitism at our own peril, and the peril is that we, too, fall into absurdity. Indeed, the whole subject of the nature and causation of this most noxious component of Pound's thought invariably reveals more about the critic than it does of Pound himself. And this had been true from the beginning, when Clark Emery, the first critic to devote a whole book to the *Cantos,* spoke of "that uninvolved non-Jewish stance" held by the "analyst" who can see Pound's "alleged" anti-Semitism from several perspectives:

> 1. He is, without qualification, anti-Semitic.
> 2. He is primarily anti-monotheist and therefore . . . both anti-Christian and anti-Semitic.
> 3. He is not anti-Semitic but anti-usural. [And several other possibilities.]

This was written before the publication of the radio speeches when Pound's anti-Semitism seemed ambiguous and ill-defined, at least to those who were unfamiliar (and apparently to many who weren't) with his papers on money and social credit.

The choices that Emery offers are, I suppose, as harmless as they are meaningless. More disconcerting is his assumption that one can't expect Jews to be rational or analytical on the subject of Pound. As it turns out, to be analytical means presenting a sanitized image of the poet and insisting on his merits. Thus Emery cannot tolerate a popular conception of Pound that may have more truth in it than his own:

> the concept of Pound as the "mad, traitorous, fascist, anti-Semitic poet" [that] has been, recently, widely disseminated. So far as the poem is concerned, my hope is that the reader will place these segments of Pound's thought in their proper relation to the other segments and to the totality of his thought and will forego preoccupation with the segments in favor of appreciation of the whole. (69)

Isn't this the real question at hand, here begged? Is anti-Semitism a mere segment among other segments that the rational critic will not dwell upon so that he can appreciate the whole; or is it rather a toxin that pollutes everything with which it comes in contact and infects the whole? I'm not so sure we can excuse Emery on the grounds that his remarks are limited to the poetry where anti-Semitic remarks are scattered throughout the text and do not hold the central position that they do in the radio speeches.

And what of these speeches? I understand that their general editor, Leonard B. Doob, had to be persuaded to undertake the task, all the more reason for his attempt to bring a scrupulous scholarship to the materials. Too scrupulous, perhaps. One of the more remarkable sections of this depressing publication is a series of appendices that convey not a thought or a hint bearing upon Pound's guilt or innocence or any other subject in which "relevance" is a criterion for inclusion. We are given, for example, "Number of Themes in Critics' Excerpts," and "Number of References in Critics' Excerpts," none of which has anything but a statistical existence in which number appears in inverse ratio to the degree of logic or common sense.

4. Anti-Semitism and the Monological Gentile

It is not that Doob is trying to claim for Pound a valid mode of either mathematical precision or intuitionist reasoning—he is not an apologist or even a declared supporter. On the contrary, what he is doing is attempting to demonstrate his own commitment to analytical objectivity—as if such objectivity could be separated from its political context and shared by all Pound scholars of good will, anti-Semitic or not. In other words, he uses the language of scholarship not to convey authentic scholarly knowledge but rather to give the allusion that his remarks are of fundamental scholarly interest, when, in fact, they are not even interesting from a methodological point of view. Appendix 4, entitled innocuously enough, "Style and Techniques," discusses what it calls the *qualitative* rather than the quantitative devices that Pound "employed intentionally or not in his attempt to influence his audience." Doob here launches into a discussion of rhetorical devices that could have appeared in any primer:

> Within a broadcast Pound's approach was perfectly straight-forward. Before writing a script he must have had a central idea that he immediately expressed either in the title he gave the speech or its first sentence or paragraph. Then he elaborated this theme by giving illustrations, by recounting anecdotes, certainly by injecting his own philosophy of values and economics.... By and large, he never wandered over an ideological map. (437)

Is there really nothing offensive in this image of a scholarly Pound going about his business of constructing a fascist radio speech, an activity made to seem so familiar that it could not possibly be connected to sinister forces either political or psychological? And what of that addendum about Pound's never wandering over an ideological map? Is this Doob's way of exonerating Pound from all taint of distraction (he never wandered) or is it just a disingenuous attempt to perpetuate the image of Pound as a careful scholar and precisionist when it came to radio scripts no

Pedagogy and/or Pedagoguery:

less than to poetic texts? In any case I don't see how anyone can seriously insist that Pound was free of ideology—if he wasn't all over the ideological map he was dangerously rooted to one segment of it.

Pursuing an *ignis fatuus* of analytical objectivity, Doob remains noncommittal to the end. He presents himself as a running commentator on the devices and principles by which Pound turned cantos into radio speeches and vice versa. The image is always Pound the Rhetor; never Pound the anti-Semite or Fascist. This is not entirely so with William Chace, who in his study of the political views of Pound and Eliot is more willing to come to terms with the difficult realities. Yet even Chace does not get to the core of the problem, at least not in the passage cited by Doob, who notes with approval Chace's argument for the historical genesis of Pound's anti-Semitism.

We don't actually know whether Doob really believes that Pound's propaganda is best explained by its connection to his previous ideas on economics and history, but Chace does seem to be moving in that direction: "It is difficult to be objective about these broadcasts [he tells us], but they can be considered a demotic expression of what Pound has been saying for years." Now, why should it be so difficult to be objective about the radio speeches—and what, in fact, does it mean to be "objective" in this instance? Does it mean that one must find "good" things to say about a "bad" text? Is it "unobjective" to condemn a text completely? Or again, is objectivity simply a matter of detached explanation, with the specific assumption here being that Pound's opinions about Jews and their conspiracy to take over the world are legitimate or respectable insofar as they are relatable to a larger body of ideas, an ideology, a vision, rooted in the past?

> The opinions are old opinions. Pound sees old-fashioned "Yankee" independence and craftsmanship everywhere on the wane. [Certain] references, however, are new, those to

4. Anti-Semitism and the Monological Gentile

"the Jewspapers and worse than Jewspapers," to "Franklin Finklestein Roosevelt," to "kikes," "sheenies," and "the oily people." (Chace, 84)

So appalling and mindless are the new references, that no tradition, no past could ever lend them sufficient dignity to be anything more than words scrawled on the wall of a men's john. At least they would never have appeared on Mantegna's wall, of which Pound had a much clearer vision in his younger days.

Pound's anti-Semitism and the language of propaganda in which it is couched was probably explained most convincingly by his daughter, Mary de Rachewiltz, when she wrote, *"Lord of his work and master of utterance*—he was that no longer. And perhaps he sensed it and all the more strongly clung to the utterances of Confucius, because his own tongue was tricking him, running away with him, leading him into excess, away from his pivot, into blind spots. I know no other explanation for some of his violent expressions—perhaps he felt the exasperation at not being able to get his real meaning across" (Rachewiltz, 173–74).[3]

Meaning in Pound's writings is countered by nonmeaning, lyric by diatribe, pedagogy by pedagoguery, education by propaganda, Confucian order by anti-Semitic violence, Logos by anti-Logos. The antithetical principle is what Oppen was referring to when he talked about "obscurity" and the unavoidable "messiness" into which many of his poems fell—all opposed to the "lyric valuable," the poem or object in full clarity. It's what Rakosi meant when he explained the "counter-will," a conception he had picked up from Otto Rank; and it's what was *à rebours* in Zukofsky as he pursued, often in vain, the clarifying form.

I hope I will not be accused of trying to confound the conventions of interpretive criticism; it is precisely these conventions (specifically, the ideals of objectivity and analytic detachment) that are most vulnerable to the kind of disruption or distortion that anti-Semitism usually brings about. Even so common a distinction as that which Doob, ever seeking objectivity, makes between friendly and unfriendly critics does not bear scrutiny. Just what is it that the critic counted friendly is friendly to? The broadcast? Pound's anti-Semitism in general? His poetry? His whole range of thought exclusive of his anti-Semitism? Does unfriendly mean merely unsympathetic or does it have attached to it a stigma of prejudice wherein the critic is judged to be a benighted anti-Poundian from whom we can expect nothing but hostility to the broadcasts, the Cantos, and so forth? I admit that all of this would be hair-splitting were it not for the fact that Doob seems only a step away from Emery's suggestion that Jews are incapable of making trustworthy (objective) statements about Pound or his broadcasts in particular. Conversely, only a non-Jew would be able to respond to the broadcasts with detachment—that is, in whatever way would allow their good and bad points to be indicated.

But, as I have argued, all such distinctions become meaningless or irrelevant when applied to the speeches. For taken as an anti-Semitic phenomenon in itself this collection cannot be said to show strength of thought or language here, weakness and failure there. It is *in toto* a debilitation of thought and language into anti-logos or "mono-logos," the expression of a mind negating itself—of the Master of Utterance dominated by his tongue and the Lord of Words become a false god.

15 Hemingstein
The Way It Wasn't

Only Leslie Fiedler would have the combination of gall and imagination to argue that, in the "creation of images of Jewishness," Ernest Hemingway was superior to Ludwig Lewisohn, and that Robert Cohn "is a realer Jew than any of Lewisohn's; that he is the product of anti-Semitic malice rather than love is from a literary point of view irrelevant. For better or for worse, it is Hemingway's image of the Jew which survives the twenties: an overgrown boyscout and hangdog lover—an outsider still, even among outsiders, and self-imposed exile" (Fiedler, 66).

I frankly don't see how "overgrown boyscout" or "hangdog lover" can, without total violation of common sense, be said to represent a "realer" Jew than the one found in Lewisohn's fiction or in that of any other Jewish writer.[1] The creation of images of Jewishness presupposes that no archetype or platonic image exists, that the defining qualities of character originate in the imagination and experience of the writer. In telling us, then, that Robert Cohn is an expression of Hemingway's "anti-Semitic malice" and at the same time a relatively realistic image of Jewishness, Fiedler seems to be unconsciously assenting to Jean-Paul Sartre's specious argument that the Jew is an invention of the anti-Semite.

Basically sympathetic, Sartre, as we have seen, falls short of the realistic characterization of Jewishness and often ends up with stereotypes so damaging as to smack of anti-Semitism themselves. What, then, can be expected of Hemingway, who is "explicitly" anti-Semitic? And to what extent is *The Sun Also Rises* affected, as a literary masterpiece, by the obvious anti-Semitism centered upon a minor character or rather a character that seems to have been created as an expression of the author's contempt for Jews?

Now, Carlos Baker has argued that "Hemingway's anti-Semitism was no more than skin deep; it was mainly a verbal habit rather than a persistent theme as in Pound." He points to occurrences in Hemingway's letters of terms like "frog, wop, jig, and kike" and deems it regrettable that Hemingway was "born into a time when such epithets were ... commonplace." Well, if this is so, Hemingway, the writer, who placed such great store on a disciplined, laconic style that expressed feelings "truly," should have been above using these commonplaces, especially when they demeaned both the user and the object of his scorn alike. And how deep is "skin deep" when it comes to anti-Semitism? Tattoos are also only skin deep and they can be immutable, vivid, and potent in their effect upon the wearer.

I am not, however, saying that this is the case with Hemingway. Moreover, I see little value in trying to determine with what degree of anti-Semitism Hemingway, brought before some inverse Inquisition, can be charged. What I am interested in is, first of all, what Hemingway in creating a Jewish character takes Jewishness to be; second, what he wants his reader to think and feel about that character; and finally, how the Jewish motif, if there is one, is related to the main themes of the novel. The answers to these questions will provide a specific—indeed unique—context in which the concepts of monologism, of *distance* and *relation*, are worked out in terms of anti-Semitism.

Baker has already replied to the first two of these problems:

4. Anti-Semitism and the Monological Gentile

> When accused of having pilloried Harold Loeb as Robert Cohn in *The Sun Also Rises*, [Hemingway] rejoined that there was no law against portraying a bounder and a cad as such merely because he happened to be of Jewish extraction. (*Letters*, xvix)

I'd like to know what Hemingway meant here by "happened to be." Is he suggesting that Loeb (or Cohn) was a bounder and a cad and the fact that he was Jewish had nothing to do with these traits? If so, why should there be in the novel any reference at all to Cohn's Jewishness or why indeed give the obnoxious character a Jewish name? "Who happens to be of Jewish extraction" means one thing when it refers to an actual person; quite another when it refers to a fictional character, for whom, if the writer is in complete control, there are no "happened to be's"; there is only the necessity of the moral and aesthetic order in which everything has meaning and everything is interrelated. In so carefully designed a novel as *The Sun Also Rises*, therefore, it is unlikely that the Jewishness of Robert Cohn is mere happenstance, an isolated characteristic written into the novel only because the model "happened to be Jewish."

Unfortunately, Harold Loeb, whom Sartre would no doubt have counted an "inauthentic Jew," was not the material from which Hemingway might fashion a verisimilar image of Jewishness, if such in fact was his aim. The reason for this is that his flight from his situation as a Jew was so definitive that Loeb seems no longer aware he ever was a Jew. I don't think there is a single reference to Jews or Judaism in his autobiography, *The Way It Was*.

A particularly telling passage in this work reveals the way Loeb sees himself and his situation. He and Duff Twitchell (Brett Ashley of the novel) have gone off on a two-week romance to St. Jean-de-Luz in southern France. On the train down, this conversation takes place:

> "There's something about Americans I don't understand," [says Duff].

> I suspected that what puzzled Duff was our approach to life. . . .
> "You English," I said, "break away usually for personal reasons. . . . With us Americans—those of my generation at least—it was more than that. Some kind of change took place that affected nearly everyone. The older people drank more openly and went in for dancing. Young women discarded corsets, drank cocktails, and smoked cigarettes. . . . A few of us took more drastic action. Not only did we leave home and parents, but we also threw out nearly everything they believed in. (259-60)

The "you English" and "us Americans" tells us all we need to know about Loeb's self-image; he is wholly the spokesman for the nation and if he identifies himself with any single group it is simply that of his generation. And Duff accepts him on that basis, telling him, "you have a nice voice, darling, an exuberant, confident voice"—the voice of an American, in other words, certainly not that of a Jew. "Not only did we leave home and parents, but we also threw out nearly everything they believed in." In more ways than one!

Reflecting on the imminent demise of his friendship with Hemingway as the two of them seek a suitable location for their fist fight, a fight that never takes place, Loeb makes this interpretation of his life:

> It was my pattern, I felt, slowly, gradually, to acquire a friend and then have him turn in an instant into a bitter lashing enemy. It happened at Princeton and Mohegan, and in The Sunwise Turn [a book shop that Loeb owned and operated]. Even in marriage. There was something about me. I felt excruciatingly lonely. (296)

When he expresses befuddlement over the situation at Princeton, he seems to ignore Jake's account of Cohn's experience with anti-Semitism while a student there. In other words, it doesn't even occur to Loeb that being a Jew is part of his "mysterious" pattern.

4. Anti-Semitism and the Monological Gentile

Now, there is nothing in his autobiography about being a boxing champion at Princeton, although Loeb did learn to box. This is a highly significant discrepancy: Jake tells us that Cohn learned to box "to counteract the feeling of inferiority and shyness he had felt on being treated as a Jew.... There was a certain inner comfort in knowing he could knock down anyone who was snooty to him, although being very shy and a thoroughly nice boy, he never fought except in the gym."

It turns out that these are Hemingway's own feelings and that Cohn has been created to express them. In reality it is Hemingway who is the boxer and when he challenges Loeb, Loeb does not exactly respond like a champion: "I was scared, not shaken or panicky, but just plain scared. I had boxed enough with him to know that he could lick me easily; his forty pound advantage was just too much.... I could not hope to outbox him." Cohn's abject apology to Jake for having knocked him down was in reality Hemingway's apology to Loeb:

> Dear Harold:
> I was terribly tight and nasty to you last night and I don't want you to go away with that nasty insulting lousiness as the last thing of the fiestas. I wish I could wipe out all the mean-ness and I suppose I can't but this is to let you know I am thoroly ashamed of the way I acted and the stinking, unjust uncalled for things I said. (*Letters*, 166)

The language of this note invites study, for however contrite Hemingway felt, his apology is still a caricature of self-recrimination and there is clearly a tone of condescension—that of adult speaking to child—in the mannered simplifications of the diction and vocabulary.

When he was in high school, Carlos Baker tells us, Hemingway and two of his friends, Lloyd Golder and Ray Ohlsen, became mock Jews (within the limits of the mores of the day): Hemingstein, Goldberg, and Cohn. Hemingway,

Baker relates, "drew three circles in yellow chalk on [each of their] locker doors and said they represented a pawn shop" (*Life*, 19). Hemingstein is sophomore Hemingway's image of the Jew, stereotypical and about as authentic as the name (though we wonder at the irony of his choosing precisely that suffix). But isn't Hemingstein also Hemingway's alter-ego, a persona through whom he can present the Jew as a clown or in fact as anything he wishes? And perhaps in a more meaningful way, Robert Cohn is Jake's alter-ego, the Jew who though characterized as an oaf and a clown achieves with Brett what is forever denied Jake.

It may be stretching things to suggest that Jake has Jewish characteristics that make Cohn a "brother," but his situation is not wholly dissimilar. Loeb was upset with Cohn's crying so much in the novel and Hemingway told him that he (Loeb) himself cried too much for a man. Well, Jake Barnes does a lot of crying, too, the only difference being that Cohn is visible and Jake has only Brett to observe him. And this is the way the group defines a Jew: not by his tears and suffering as such but by their visibility, which is nothing but an embarrassment. That Jake's agonies have an identical source is of no consequence either to Jake or to the group in their treatment of Cohn, who no matter what he does can never receive the acceptance that Jake does. Cohn is not the brother but a rival, not a true alter-ego but a scapegoat who suffers in public what Jake suffers in private. Accordingly, it would be *de trop* for Jake to meet Cohn on the level of I-Thou and we find, in all their relations, Jake's attempt to maintain dominance and distance. With one notable exception the struggle is verbal, and Cohn is disadvantaged from the beginning.

As the narrator Jake is a monologist—that is, he is in full control of how Cohn is presented, and we are constrained to accept the "graven image" of him that he creates. He is also a monologist as a participant in the action and adept enough that Cohn doesn't realize that he is being patronized or insulted. Until the crisis with Brett, Jake speaks

158   4. Anti-Semitism and the Monological Gentile

with mixed emotions and his witticism at Jewish expense doesn't cut deep. When he tells us, for example, how Cohn's coach overmatched him and got his nose broken, he can't resist adding that it gave Cohn a certain satisfaction "and it certainly improved his nose." Not very insulting but not very original either. Jake, however, does overreach himself in the scene in which Cohn sees Brett for the first time:

> I saw Robert Cohn looking at her. He looked a great deal as his compatriate must have looked when he saw the promised land. Cohn, of course, was much younger. But he had that look of eager, deserving expectation.

What look of eager, deserving expectation? Is this comparison of the smitten Cohn to Moses looking on Canaan an example of Hemingstein's wit or is Jake trying to be clever to mask other feelings? Thus, Jake continues with this seemingly appreciative but detached description that does in fact have beneath it a painful relationship:

> Brett was damned good-looking. She wore a slipover jersey sweater and a tweed skirt, and her hair was brushed like a boy's. She started all that. She was built with curves like the hull of a racing yacht and you missed none of it with that wool jersey. (22)

Obviously, Jake has the same look on his face as have Cohn and his "compatriate" and we know that he will never see Canaan either.

As I have said, Jake cannot always withstand the pressures of his suppressed and unrequited (unrequitable) love. At one point in the narration, he actually takes off his mask and states without any kind of evasion or wit what his true feelings are:

> I was blind, unforgivingly jealous of what had happened to him [Cohn]. The fact that I took it as a matter of course

did not alter that any. I certainly did hate him. I do not think I ever really hated him until he had that little spell of superiority.... (99)

This kind of lapse is rare for Jake, who, most of the time, can manipulate our feelings even with the slightest of touches. Here is part of an argument with Cohn over Brett:

> "You asked me what I knew about Brett Ashley."
> "I didn't ask you to insult her."
> "Oh, go to hell."
> He stood up from the table his face white, and stood there white and angry behind the little plates of hors d'oeuvres. (39)

I don't deny that his response is excessive but after those little plates of hors d'oeuvres what chance does Cohn have of appearing anything but a clown. Thus even though Jake eventually apologizes ("I've got a nasty tongue"), he still emerges looking more sophisticated, more commanding, and much tougher than his adversary.

Now, Hemingway is, to put it crudely, always loading the dice against Cohn and Loeb. For instance, he will put words and opinions into Cohn's mouth that were originally expressed by another person, as in the episode in which Cohn tries in vain to get Jake to go to South America with him. Note the patronizing tone and in-group wit by which Jake keeps himself on top and Cohn off-balance:

> "Hello, Robert," I said. "Did you come in to cheer me up?" [Facetious from the beginning: Cohn is being characterized as the last person that could cheer up Jake. Why, incidentally, does Jake always address Cohn as Robert, and not by his diminutive? After all, he calls Gorton "Bill" and Campbell "Mike," etc. "Bob," I suppose, would be too familiar for someone Jake will never fully accept or allow any of the intimacies of genuine friendship ("You're really about the best friend I have, Jake." "God help you," I thought.).

4. Anti-Semitism and the Monological Gentile

That Jake is sensitive to how names are used is made apparent when he says to Cohn, who is trying to apologize for having hit him, "Don't call me Jake." To return to the quotation:]

"Would you like to go to South America, Jake?"
"No."
"Why not?"
"I don't know. I never wanted to go. Too expensive. You can see all the South Americans you want in Paris anyway."
"They're not the real South Americans."
"They look awfully real to me." (9)

What Jake is actually saying here is that only a hopelessly naïve romantic, somebody who had read a book like Hudson's *The Purple Land* and believed it, would ever want to visit so "obvious" a place as South America. Here is an exchange between Loeb and Duff during their trip. Loeb asks Duff whether she's ever read Hudson's *Green Mansions*, which he confesses to having enjoyed for its mysteries even though he has, as Duff has accused him, too much faith in logic:

"I never read *Green Mansions*. Didn't it take place in South America?"
"Physically," I said, "but it could have been anywhere."
"I have often thought about South America," Duff said. "Should we go there, darling? To a strange land, all new and different. To live as you want to live. Take a boat and go just like that?"
"No," I said without hesitation, "not South America." (274-75)

This *is* confusion! Loeb, the supposed model for Cohn, decidedly not wishing to go to South America, with all its "romance" and "mystery," and seeing himself as a man of reason and logic; Duff, a nihilist except when in bed, vaguely dreaming of a voyage to South America, briefly taking, in effect, the role of Cohn. "Maybe you are not one of us after all," she says momentously, but adds, "Yet you are a dear." "Maybe you are not one of us" because "you have such faith in what the world calls logic"—is what she is saying here, and in committing the group to magic and mystery plays havoc with some of the most cherished values of *The Sun Also Rises*.

What happens in the novel is that Hemingway, through Jake, makes Cohn the sole spokesman for naïve romanticism and it is Duff's feelings, not Loeb's, that Cohn elaborates. The whole episode is designed to demonstrate once again Cohn's naïvité and sentimentality. But the ideas and feelings in question are being ridiculed not because they are inherently ludicrous, but because they are being expressed by Cohn. If, having read Hudson, Brett had asked Jake to take her to South America, we can be sure that Jake would have had the tickets within the hour and they would have left on the next boat-train. Cohn, of course, doesn't have a chance; not only is he refused with condescension, but his persistence gains him the ultimate dismissal: "He had a hard Jewish stubborn streak," says Jake. So much for South America. And so much for Cohn, who always ends up a kind of Hemingstein and a foil for Jake. Accordingly, his Jewishness is as skin deep as Hemingway's anti-Semitism, as true to life as a Jewish pawnshop in a high school locker.

16 The Polyphonic Persecution of Yakov Bok

In one of his essays on Jewish-American fiction, Philip Roth cites the tendency of Saul Bellow to associate the "Jewish Jew" with "the struggles of ethical Jewhood" and the "non-Jewish Jew," "and the Gentile with the release of appetite and aggression." In Bernard Malamud, Roth says, "these tendencies are so sharply and schematically present as to give [his] novels the lineaments of moral allegory" (*Reading Myself*, 286). Thus, for Malamud, "the Jew is innocent, passive, virtuous, and this to the degree that he defines himself or is defined by others as a Jew; the Gentile, on the other hand, is characteristically corrupt, violent, and lustful, particularly when he enters a room or a store or a cell with a Jew in it" (287). It is Roth's opinion that such "evangelic simplifications" are usually not convincing, but in Malamud, whose imagination is folkloric and didactic, the more they are adhered to, the more successful they are.

This is a provocative theory, but like many such theories, its powers of illumination are considerably diminished when we take a closer look at the text. Roth deals mainly with *The Assistant*, but if any book seems to bear out his thesis, it is *The Fixer*, in which the Jewish hero, Yakov Bok, survives two years of false imprisonment by a Russian society wholly permeated by a rabid medieval anti-Semitism. Peasant, merchant, clergyman, soldier, bureaucrat, laborer, the Tsar himself, all stand in implacable loathing of Jews as a whole and of the one Jew, whom they believe, on the flimsiest of evidence, has committed so-called ritual murder to obtain the blood of a Christian child for ceremonial purposes.

"I know of no [other] serious authors," says Roth, "whose novels have chronicled physical brutality and fleshly mortification in such detail and at such length, and who likewise have taken a single defenseless innocent and constructed almost an entire book out of the relentless violation suffered by that character at the hands of cruel and perverse captors" (291). This is true; furthermore, Malamud says nothing about the support that Mendel Beiliss, Bok's real-life model, receives from the press and the intelligentsia nor does he give any indication that Beiliss was eventually acquitted.[1] The only difficulty is that Bok is not a Jewish Jew, if by that we mean a Torah-reading Jew who has a strong faith in God and diligently performs the rituals. Even before his troubles with the State, Bok revealed himself to be a less than avid lover of God as this conversation with his father-in-law makes clear:

> "Yakov," said Shmuel passionately, "don't forget your God!"
> "Who forgets who?" the fixer said angrily. "What do I get from him but a bang on the head and a stream of piss in my face. So what's there to be worshipful about?"
> "Don't talk like a meshummed [convert]. Stay a Jew, Yakov, don't give up our God." (17)

Nor after over two years of prison life has he been led to change his mind:

> "I want no part of God. When you need him most, he's farthest away. Enough is enough."
> "Yakov," said Shmuel . . . "we're not Jews for nothing.

> Without God we can't live.... He's all we have but who wants more?"
> "Me. I'll take misery but not forever."
> "For misery don't blame God."
> "I blame him for not existing. Or if he does it's on the moon or stars but not here."

"If you don't hear His voice," Shmuel replies, "so let Him hear yours. 'When prayers go up blessings descend.'" But Yakov will have none of it:

> Scorpions descend, hail, fire, sharp rocks, excrement. For all that I don't need God's help, the Russians are enough. All right, once I used to talk to him and answer myself.... whatever I said, he never answered me. Silence I now give back. (256–57)

The meaning of Bok's ultimate triumph over the system—that is, his survival—is not at all the same as it would have been had he been a man of faith and an observant Jew. His triumph could then have signified the collective victory of the Jews in their ability to endure. But Bok is, rather, an existential Jew, isolated in a meaningless universe and at the mercy of a murderously hostile Other that includes God, if he is in fact still "alive."[2] Far from being the hero of a Jewish morality play, he rather resembles Camus's Meursault (*The Stranger*), another man victimized by a society intolerant of "strangeness." Brought to trial for killing an Arab, Meursault is in fact condemned for his tactless honesty and general apathy, epitomized by his failure to show grief over the death of his mother. The French justice system, in its treatment of a nonconformist *colon* in pre–World War II Algeria, bears a marked resemblance to the Russian system in its treatment of a Jew under the tsars [Meursault is recalling the Prosecutor's summation]:

> Really, he said, I had no soul, there was nothing human about me, not one of those moral qualities which normal

men possess had any place in my mentality. . . . in a criminal court the wholly passive ideal of tolerance must give place to a sterner, loftier ideal, that of justice. Especially when this lack of every decent instinct is such as that of the man before you, a menace to society. (Camus, 127)

Meursault experiences a kind of revelation through which he identifies himself with an absurd universe (laying his heart open to the *benign indifference* of the world) and declares himself happy in the feeling of liberation that knowledge of approaching death gives him. A stoic who can announce that even if he were compelled to live in a tree trunk with nothing to do but gaze up at a patch of sky, he would have become used to it by degrees, Meursault goes to his death with his integrity and dignity intact.

Like Meursault, Bok is a loner, all the more so for not being able to make a philosophic adjustment to the absurdity facing him. He can make no identification of himself with a "tenderly indifferent" world and is thrown back upon his own intellectual resources to explain his position to himself and to seek some kind of reconciliation:

> There was no "reason," there was only their plot against a Jew, any Jew; he was the accidental choice for the sacrifice. He would be tried because the accusation had been made, there didn't have to be another reason. Being born a Jew meant being vulnerable to history, including its worst errors. (155)

The world offers no brotherly (*si fraternel enfin*) reflection to Bok as it does to Meursault; that is why, unlike Meursault, he initially falls into unrelieved despair:

> He felt entrapped, abandoned, helpless. He had disappeared from the world and nobody he could call friend knew it. Nobody. . . . In a philosophical moment he cursed history, anti-Semitism, fate, and even, occasionally, the Jews. "Who will help me?" he cried out. . . . (155)

4. Anti-Semitism and the Monological Gentile

The essential conflict in the novel, then, is not simply between the good Jew and the evil gentile but between the seemingly unheroic and vulnerable average man and a society that is bent upon turning him into a thing or thoroughly depriving him of his humanity. Bok has none of the symbolism of Meursault. Possessed of "lucidity," "a desire to use up all that the world offers him," and other qualities that have special significance in Camus's view of the universe, Meursault goes to his death feeling superior to his fate. (Interestingly enough, Meursault did in fact commit the crime of which he is accused, though he seems to be exonerated by the author on the grounds that, having no motive and merely yielding to the "Absurd," he was less blameworthy than a society that would impose the death penalty.)

Calling out in despair for help, Bok elicits compassion or pity, not admiration. But he survives and Meursault doesn't. Furthermore, Meursault's attitude upon his death is solely a personal triumph and of no social consequence, whereas Bok is eventually able to commit himself to an idea that, while remaining a part of his own perspective of his situation, is wholly unselfish. Thus, held in almost total isolation, surrounded by hostile functionaries, Bok alone can give meaning to his meaningless, arbitrary ordeal.[3] Even though he basically is not a symbol but a victim, he comes to the undoubtedly correct conclusion that he will be seen as a symbol by the anti-Semitic public:

> To the goyim what one Jew is is what they all are. If the fixer stands accused of murdering one of their children, so does the rest of the tribe. Since the crucifixion the crime of the Christ-killer is the crime of all Jews. . . . Those Jews who escape [atrocity] with their lives live in memory's eternal pain. So what can Yakov Bok do about it? All he can do is not make things worse. . . . If God's not a man he has to be. Therefore he must endure to the trial and let them confirm his innocence by their lies. He has no future but hold on, wait it out. . . .

"I'll live," he shouts out in his cell. "I'll wait, I'll come to my trial." (274–75)

This is not the kind of individualistic and romantic heroism that commentators like Bruno Bettelheim saw, or thought they saw, in the German concentration camps. And it is in arguing against Bettelheim that Terrence Des Pres, in *The Survivor*, states that not self-orientation but socially directed activity made survival possible. Organization, group action, political awareness—the presence of an underground resistance force—would, of course, be more effective than isolated individual heroism in preserving life in the camps, even if that meant creating leeway where none existed. According to Des Pres, what makes social action possible under such conditions as the Nazis imposed upon the prisoners is a "need to help others," a tendency toward solidarity, that was just as strong as, if not stronger than, the brute will for self-preservation alone that led to the fierce, often mortal, competition of one victim against another.

Kept incommunicado by his captors, Bok, in morally justifying his refusal to confess guilt to a crime he never committed, chooses, solely on his own individual responsibility, solidarity with the Jews in their historical suffering; it doesn't matter that he believes himself to be only "half" Jewish. Half or whole, he stands by his resolution. Thus Bok's narration ends as he is enroute to the trial; this is all that is necessary for him to meet his obligation to his decision. He has faith that the trial itself will bear testimony for him and ultimately, to go beyond fiction to reality, it does.

Whatever his reasons for not attempting suicide, for not confessing to the charges against him, for living to bear witness to his experience, and, finally, for preventing another pogrom against the Jews, Bok must live his life in the total isolation, both spiritual and actual, in which his jailers keep him. He is subjected to physical torture and constant harassment, one of the worst ordeals residing in the fact that he is never allowed to fully express himself, to speak without being interrupted, indeed to be even listened to. Whether or not this is by design, monologue is the natural medium of authority and grotesque monologue the medium of oppression. Bok's instincts to communicate—to find someone whom he can address as Thou—even if that means no more than banging out morse code with a shoe against the cell wall—are repeatedly frustrated.[4] Conversely, he is confronted with endless reports, both oral and written, all of which are based upon distorted evidence, false or irrelevant testimony, hearsay, and emotional or subjective opinion—all masked by a legalistic diction that seems to give them the ring of truth. In anti-Semitism, the many voices of "polyphonic" Russia speak as one voice or monologue in which Bok is condemned before he is tried. (Only one gentile, Bibikov, the Investigating Magistrate, demurs and his voice is extinguished.)

Through all this, however, Bok never sees himself as a saint or a hero; he wants cessation of suffering, not martyrdom; freedom, not canonization. Thus, when in an imaginary conversation, the Tsar asks him whether suffering has not taught him the meaning of mercy, Bok replies "Excuse me, Your Majesty, but what suffering has taught me is the uselessness of suffering" (333).[5]

Rather, it is the Tsar who would be the martyr, telling Bok, who fantasizes that he is about to shoot him, "I am the victim, the sufferer for my poor people. What will be, will be." This is precisely what Bok is not; the Tsar's response is nothing but the sentimentality of a man who has no idea what real suffering is and therefore no idea of what he has inflicted upon the Jews. But neither is Bok the Avenging Angel bringing retribution to the destroyers of the children of Israel. Far from being associated with the ultimate forces of the universe, he's simply a man with a gun, who, having been singled out as a Jew and badly brutalized, fires for reasons neither sentimental nor grandiose:

This is . . . for the prison, the poison, the six daily searches. It's for Bibikov and Kogin and for a lot more that I won't even mention. . . .
What the Tsar deserves is a bullet in the gut. Better him than us. (334)

This is not, I repeat, a metaphysical rebellion; it is personal revenge, an act emanating from frustration and anger over what has been done to him and to his friends. Indeed the very conversation he has been holding with the Tsar is itself a part of the tyranny of communication that has been a major cause of his frustration and anger from the time of his arrest.

Bok shoots the Tsar not only because he holds him responsible for past crimes, but because the Tsar is not really listening to him—in fact is incapable of understanding or appreciating what Bok is trying to tell him. The Tsar speaks in "a quiet voice with moving eloquence," a bad sign from the start since eloquence is an important trait of the monologist and that is exactly what the Tsar turns out to be. There can be no dialogue in a state in which atrocity is not only legal but demanded by the authorities. Thus the Tsar enters into a long, rambling soliloquy in which he touches upon his hatred of Jews and his revulsion over their blood rites, his sorrows over his son's hemophilia, his good fortune in having healthy daughters, and other such matters, all of them being wholly irrelevant to the issue that Bok, who is silent until spoken to, wishes to discuss.

Monologism is (as I have said) a prerogative of authority and particularly of anti-Semitic authority. Unchallenged or ineffectively challenged, the speaker pursues whatever arguments, whatever lies or half-truths, best serve him. Here is the episode in which Grubeshov, the Prosecuting Attorney, is trying to talk Bok into confessing:

"I am innocent," the fixer shouted hoarsely.
"No Jew is innocent, least of all a ritual assassin. [Begs

170   4. Anti-Semitism and the Monological Gentile

the question] Furthermore, it is known you are an agent of
the Jewish Kabal, the secret Jewish international government which is engaged in a subterranean conspiracy with
the World Zionist Organization, the Alliance of Herzl, and
the Russian Freemasons. [Multiple lies or else Grubeshov
presents superstition for fact, paranoia for detachment, hysteria for analytical rigor] We also have reason to believe that
your masters [question begging, again] are dickering with
the British to help you overthrow the legitimate Russian
government and make yourselves rulers of our land and
people [no evidence offered for any of this except the *Protocols of the Elders of Zion*. By now Grubeshov is so far from
the point that he elicits an outburst from the fixer: "I am
not a revolutionist. I am an inexperienced man. Who knows
about such things?" Bok might as well be talking to the
walls.

"You can deny it all you want, we know the truth," Grubeshov shouted. "The Jews dominate the world and we feel
ourselves under their yoke. I personally feel myself under
the power of the Jews; under the power of Jewish thought,
under the power of the Jewish press.... I am a Russian
patriot! I love the Russian Tsar!"

Yakov stared miserably at the indictment papers. (225–26)

All the state functionaries and representatives of established power have their elegant anti-Semitic monologues by
which in lieu of real evidence they hope to intimidate Bok
into confessing. We are even shown the text of a letter to
Bok from Marfa Golov, the victim's mother, urging his repentance. And the church appears in the form of a monk
who, as a "specialist" in Judaica, gives a long, specious, but
warmly received, account of Jewish blood-rites. All means
of communication being in the hands of those who for
personal, political, social, or moral reasons are trying to
destroy him, it is little wonder that Bok, a pariah even before his troubles, can find no meaning in his suffering.

I have been taking the question of suffering—that is, the
question of the value of trying to find meaning and worth

in suffering—in its "metaphysical" sense; that is, as something apart from Bok's practical use of suffering, which he accepts in order to have his day in court. Suffering may be endured to reach a higher goal or to fulfill a specific aim; one accepts it because one must; that is not to say that one is romantically glorifying it or even justifying its existence. In no sense does Bok see anything positive—for instance, self-ennoblement or self-growth—in what he has had to endure. We are left with the impression that whatever his survival gained for him in terms of personal stature, he would rather never have left the shtetl in the first place. And who are we to blame him?

Notes
Works Cited
Index

Notes

Introduction

1. I am, of course, paraphrasing the Heraclitean fragment well-known to readers of both Buber and T. S. Eliot: "Although the Word is common to all, most men act as each had a private vision of his own."
2. Though he's never called it such, Saul Bellow, for instance, shows a keen awareness of monologism in the sense in which I've been using the term. *Mr. Sammler's Planet* opens with this reflection by the hero: "Intellectual man has become an explaining creature. Fathers to children, wives to husbands, lecturers to listeners, experts to laymen, colleagues to colleagues, doctors to patients, man to his own soul, explained.... For the most part, in one ear and out the other" (3–4). The soul is not interested in knowing the "roots of this, the causes of the other, the source of events, the history, the structure, the reason why." This knowledge belongs to the intellect and the realm of Buber's I-It; the soul has its own "natural Knowledge," eschews explanation, and seeks the dialogical.

I'm not saying that Buber in any way influenced Bellow. To the contrary, we find the hero in *Herzog* associating Buber with his detested rival, Valentin Gersbach, who brings him several of Buber's books to read: *"I'm sure you know the views of Buber* [he writes in one of his many letters]. *It is wrong to turn a man (a subject) into a thing (an object). By means of spiritual dialogue, the I-It relationship becomes an I-Thou relationship. God comes and goes in man's soul. And men come and go in each other's souls. Sometimes they come and go in each other's beds, too. You have dialogue with a man, you have inter-*

course with his wife. . . . And somehow it all gets translated into religious depth" (83–84). The primary intention here is to point up Gersbach's hypocrisy and his violation of the very principles he would have Herzog study. But it also seems that Buber's philosophy itself is an object of irony. The motif reappears and it is clear that Herzog in a *reductio ad absurdum* identifies Buber with adultery: "I see that Val taped a program. . . . What did he call it? 'Hasidic Judaism.' Martin Buber, *I and Thou*. Still the Buber kick! Maybe he wants to swap wives with a rabbi. He'll work his way round from 'I and Thou' to 'Me and You'—'You and Me, Kid!' "

Whatever his opinion of Buber, however, Bellow can be interpreted in Buberian terms without doing violence to his intentions. Kegan, for instance, sees in Augie March "a man of ecstasy, of *hitlahabut*, Hasid, and hallower of the world around him"; that is, he sees Augie as the embodiment of a Buberian/Hasidic ideal (71). Accordingly, he argues that Henderson "has found the rhythm of the living universe. . . . In tune, thus, with the mysterious symphony of life, [he] rests in the state of *shiflut, hitlahabut*'s transformation, feeling, just as Buber describes it, 'the universal generation as a sea, and oneself as a wave in it' " (124).

1. Sartre and the Existential Jew

1. *Being and Nothingness (L'Être et le néant)*. Tr. by Hazel Barnes. *Philosophical Library: New York, 1956, Pp. 237, 238*.
2. Sartre eventually arrived at the conception of "seriality" as a unifying principle of society, albeit a low form. Persons are united only as a series of Others by an "inert object which gathers [them] about itself, and holds them there as inert and alienated from themselves." (See Wilfred Desan, *Sartre and Marxism*, 117–18.) Seriality has something in common with Heidegger's idea of Mit-Sein (Being-With), an idea that Sartre once dismissed, along with Hegel's, for its "ontological optimism."
3. Thus in an interview with Stuart Charmé, Arlette Elkaim-Sartre, "Sartre's [Adopted] Jewish Daughter," was to say that only gradually did Sartre come to "realize that there was a positive reality to Jewishness apart from anti-Semitism." Although she was engaged in translating the Talmud, Elkaim, a *colon* who fled to France from Algeria during the war, regarded herself as fully assimilated—a nonobservant Jew who still felt certain ethnic ties (see Charmé, 27). The whole interview is illuminating.

2. Buber and the Dialogical Jew

1. Buber describes perception in the I-It relation this way: "Now with the magnifying glass of peering observation he bends over particulars and objectifies them with the field glass of remote inspection, he objectifies them and arranges them as scenery, he isolates them in observation without any feeling of their exclusiveness, or he knits them into a scheme of observation without any feeling of universality" (*I and Thou*, 29–30).

3. Stern's Silent Monologue

1. Stuart Lewis, in "Rootlessness and Alienation in Bruce Jay Friedman," traces these conditions in Stern's family life, education, religion, and human relations in general. He does not, however, look at dialogue or go into the ways in which rootlessness and alienation are dramatized by Friedman. For an interpretation of *Stern* based on Friedman's antiromantic view of love, see Max Schulz's *Radical Sophistication*.

2. It is true that the rabbi in Silvia Tennenbaum's *Rachel, the Rabbi's Wife* claims that the "*seder* is traditionally the time for family arguments . . . People have spent a whole year storing up resentments. A *seder* without an argument is like a rose without scent" (128). The rabbi is, of course, being facetious. In any case fighting is neither in spirit nor letter part of the ceremony.

3. In its admiration of the uniform and what it stands for, the congregation goes against the grain of Jewish pacifism and perhaps is even in violation of the Mosaic law against idols. Since Stern is not even a war hero, the idol is doubly false.

4. I am using the term I-I in a somewhat different sense from that used by Walter Kaufmann in the prologue to his translation of *I and Thou*. Kaufmann offers other exotic combinations (e.g., It-It), which, even though they are not in Buber, are still worth contemplating (see pp. 11–12).

4. The Tenants of Moonbloooo-ooo

1. Nazerman also suggests "Nazarene," but in no way does this name force us to interpret the pawnbroker as a "Christ figure." The irony of doing so, from both the Jewish and Christian points of view, would be too much to bear.

2. I am aware that this reading is not in accord with the standard interpretation of the conclusion, which sees a rebirth for

Nazerman ushered in by his tears and confirmed by the fact that he calls upon his nephew to help him in the shop. These are, no doubt, signs and acts of affirmation and Wallant may be telling us that Nazerman has indeed rejoined the human race or reentered the world of the living. I offer no evidence for my own view except to say that it might appeal to the skeptical reader who is unconvinced that Nazerman's rebirth will survive the shock of his assistant's death or simply finds an optimistic conclusion unrealistic and out of harmony with the mood of the novel.

5. Carnivalizing the Logos

1. For an excellent discussion of the literary versions of the *shlemiel*, see *The Shlemiel As Modern Hero* by Ruth Wisse (Chicago: University of Chicago Press, 1971).
2. I have used the enlarged version of the novel, *O Kaplan, My Kaplan!*, in which we are given a fuller view of Parkhill. That Rosten in many ways identifies himself with Parkhill adds a complication that need not distract us here. I cannot refrain from saying, however, that it is an identity altogether appropriate to the schizoid condition of the Monological Jew.

6. The New Jersey Jews and Their Pagan Gods

1. The discussion that follows for the next few pages is a digression that, being central to our overall theme, will add, I believe, to a fuller appreciation of Neil's position in the novel.
2. The sociological "type" on which the character of the overpossessive mother is modelled is described by Martha Wolfenstein, who argues that she is a product of certain conditions of shtetl life. Thus, the shtetl mother, whose duty it is to tend to all the needs of her infant son, loses him to the world of men as soon as he is of age. Nevertheless, she continues to think of him "as a helpless infant, who cannot be trusted to do anything for himself and who, if left to his own devices, will injure himself.... She is constantly worried about his health: he is in danger of catching cold from not buttoning up his jacket or not wearing his scarf or sleeping with the windows open. When she cautions him about these things, he flies into a rage, yelling that he is not a baby" (523). And so it is with all aspects of his life. (I

am indebted to Stanley Schatt, who cited Wolfenstein's study in "The Torah and the Time-Bomb: The Teaching of Jewish-American Literature Today." For an informative general discussion, see Melvin J. Friedman's "Jewish Mothers and Sons: The Expense of *Chutzpah*.")

My reading of the Jewish mother is, I must confess, in the male tradition. A well-reasoned feminist view is presented by Carol Klein in *The Woman Who Lost Her Names*, a compilation of writings by Jewish women. She argues that, as "women of all religious persuasions demand new images of themselves, Jewish women too must refuse to accept the easy generalizations that have been made about their lives. We are not the stereotypic, self-indulged daughters or grasping wives or salacious seductresses; we are not the smothering, obscenely overprotective mothers who imprison sons into cages of guilt and heterosexual conflict. These are the distorted images of male writers" (x). Granted the apparent love of caricature in Philip Roth and Bruce Jay Friedman, and perhaps even in Herbert Gold, I am not certain that the Jewish mother is as much a figment of the male writer's imagination as Klein would have us believe.

3. I am suggesting here that Portnoy's auto-eroticism is a way of defying his mother, who seems to be threatening him with castration. Actually, in Freudian thought, it is the other way around, as is made clear by the epigraph, an excerpt from the writings of Portnoy's psychoanalyst, Spielvogel: the act of auto-eroticism (with other neurotic symptoms) leads to "overriding feelings of shame and the dread of retribution, particularly in the form of castration." In any case "the symptoms can be traced to the bonds obtaining in the mother-child relationship." I don't think Roth is being satiric here, but I could be wrong.

7. David Schearl in the Polyphonic World

1. The interview is included as an appendix to Lyons's book, *Henry Roth: The Man and His Work*; the quotations are on pp. 170–71. The greater part of this study is a detailed reading of *Call It Sleep*. My chief quarrel with Lyons is, as indicated here, over the ambiguities of Roth's view of the success or failure of David Schearl to find the illumination he seeks.

2. David thinks he has found such a person in his friend, Leo

Dugovka, a Polish boy who turns out to be both anti-Semitic and exploitative.

8. Levinsky and the Language of Acquisition

1. Jules Chametzsky gives us one answer in his *Up from the Ghetto: The Fiction of Abraham Cahan*. The novel developed from some stories on "Jewish immigrant successes in American business" commissioned by *McClures*. "It was a story," says Chametzky, that Cahan knew well and which he humanized, complicated, and avoided stereotyping." Cahan's novel is in fact only one of many novels, both American and European, in which the socialist writer fails to bring to his work a socialist vision or to solve the ethical, economic, and political problems he raises in socialist terms.

2. See *Dialogue* in *Between Man and Man*, 19–20.

3. David Engel, who sees in *Levinsky* "a novel richly descriptive of that situation of history and feeling we call modernity," has this to say about the Gussie episode: "Besides the duplicity caused by sexual urgency, Levinsky's feelings are further confused by the attraction of Gussie's money and the persistence of his old-fashioned standards of sexual behavior. His attempt at cold-hearted, modern indulgence is subverted and muddled by the traditional beliefs which are still stubbornly his. Ultimately, Levinsky is left without any solid ground for his feelings, which are all, his warmth and his coolness alike, equally inauthentic." I'm not certain I understand fully what Mr. Engel is saying here but he does seem to be verging on an existentialist interpretation, especially since he writes elsewhere that "many of modernism's characteristic griefs, its feeling of loss and homelessness, as well as its brighter moments of radical liberation and invention, seem implicated in its loss of faith in teleology and its sense of discontinuity" (see Engel, 41 and 53). I agree, though Engel and I have come to this conclusion from different routes and are departing in different directions.

Sanford Marovitz traces the Oedipal implications of Levinsky's sexual development, including his condensation of all women into a single idealized figure, and goes on to make a connection between sexuality, the mastery of English, and the obtaining of power, three drives that are characteristic of life in America as well as of Levinsky's personal growth.

Chametzsky's remarks on language—particularly in regard to Levinsky's style as an expression of his emotional aridity—are a major contribution to our understanding of this motif and its significance.

9. The Family Moskat's Descent into Randomness

1. In his informative study of *The Family Moskat*, Irving Buchen writes that "Asa Heshel does indeed rot and decay in his self-sufficiency. Pursuing secular knowledge, he finds his work without end. Embracing secular messiahs and metaphysics, he regularly encounters the imperfections of mortal heavens without the consolation of divine continuity and finality. Constantly intellectualizing and philosophizing his experience, he enfeebles his heart and his power to act" (75).

10. Art and Idolatry

1. "And obscure as that heaven of the Jews, / Thy guerdon . . . Accolade thou dost bestow/ Of anonymity time cannot raise. . . ." Hart Crane was, I believe, sensitive to the problems we are discussing here.

11. Asher Lev

1. For an elaboration of this idea, see Ellen Serlen Uffen's article.

2. Thus Buber: "God has fallen into duality through the created world and its deed: into the essence of God, Elohim, which is withdrawn from the creatures, and the presence of God, the Shekina, which dwells in things, wandering, straying, scattered. Only redemption will unite the two in eternity" (*Hasidism and Modern Man*, 88).

3. S. Lillian Kremer discusses in detail the influence of James Joyce on Potok. For a less sympathetic reading of Potok's view of the Hasids and art, see Sanford Pinsker's article.

12. Reznikoff's Dispersion

1. We are reminded here of the principle that God is worshipped through His creation, which Buber ascribes to Hasidic thought (see *Hasidism and Modern Man*). Chaim Potok has argued that Buber has misinterpreted Hasidism on this crucial point (see his article, "Buber and the Jews," in *Commentary*).

13. The Objectivist Jew

1. *All, the Collected Short Poems, 1923–1958*, pp. 15–16. I have taken the liberty of omitting line numbers, which run from 110 to 117. This argument originally appeared in a somewhat different context in "Louis Zukofsky: Objectivist Poetics and the Quest for Form," *American Literature* 44, 1 (March 1972): 92–93.

2. Mary Oppen. *Meaning A Life: An Autobiography* (Santa Barbara: Black Sparrow, 1978), p. 209. This episode, along with the discussion that now follows, was originally part of an introduction to a discussion with Oppen on his early poems that appeared in *George Oppen: Man and Poet* (ed. Burton Hatlen), pp. 197ff.

3. See Hatlen's "Carl Rakosi and the Reinvention of the Epigram," in *The Collected Prose of Carl Rakosi*," 130.

14. Pedagogy and/or Pedagoguery

1. Here is a segment of Pound's translation of the passage as Marie de Rachewiltz cites it in her memoirs of her father (157): "The men of old wanting to clarify and diffuse throughout the empire that light which comes from looking straight into the heart and then acting, first set up good government in their own states, they first established order in their own families; wanting order in the home, they first disciplined themselves; desiring self discipline, they rectified their own hearts; and wanting to rectify their hearts, they sought precise verbal definitions of their inarticulate thoughts. . . ." Highly metaphorized though this translation may be, it does accurately convey the Chinese vision of a universe morally, spiritually, and physically unified. Pound's sense of unity is nowhere nearly so explicit or so comprehensive.

2. An account of Buber's theories of education appears in *Education (Rede über das Erzieherische, 1926)* and *Education of Character (Über Charaktererziehung)* both found in *Between Man and Man*. For Buber, the ideal form of education is not, of course, the lecture but the dialogue in which the full personality and character of both student and teacher are engaged.

15. Hemingstein

1. Actually Fiedler may merely be pointing out that Hemingway's idea of the Jew as depicted in Robert Cohn has made a greater impression on the public than the less talented Lewi-

sohn's figure. Thus, by default, Hemingway's image of the Jew has survived. Whatever the case, Fiedler is not very illuminating on this point.

16. The Polyphonic Persecution of Yakov Bok

1. See Grosser and Halperin for a brief account of the Beiliss affair and Samuel for a more detailed one. Beiliss was acquitted, an outcome we are in no way prepared for in Bok's case, where we are given the impression that support is limited to rare persons and that the Russian populace, virtually every man, woman, and child, is rabidly anti-Semitic. Samuel indicates that Beiliss had strong support from the liberal press, the intelligentsia, and other segments of society. In any event, the state's case was dismissed for lack of evidence.

2. Alan Friedman has asserted that "Yakov's plight, in contrast with Job's, is essentially absurd, for his world offers no possibility of a perspective in which his plight will partake of a controlling context" (297). To put it simply, without God, Bok has no authority to whom he can turn for confirmation of his behavior.

3. Friedman gives an eloquent argument for the ultimate meaningfulness of Bok's suffering (see p. 302). I can appreciate his point but I can't share his enthusiasm for Bok's affirmations. Insofar as the incarceration of Bok can be regarded as a kind of prelude to the Holocaust, I feel compelled to judge his suffering in the way that Lawrence Langer has argued we must judge that in the concentration camps: " 'Suffocation in the gas chamber' grates harshly against more consoling descriptions like 'salvation through suffering' or 'tragic insight.' But some writers on the Holocaust find it so difficult to absorb this abrasive reality, they try to adapt the facts of extermination to ideas of suffering and heroism that have governed man's secular or religious fate throughout the Judeo-Christian era. . . . Unlike the regal heroes of tragedy, [the victims of Auschwitz] possessed neither power nor freedom of choice. In this world of shrunken options, their 'defeat' can only be charitably designated as 'inhuman' " (8, 10).

Bok in fact does discover that he has a choice: he can confess and be pardoned, or he can insist on acquittal and suffer continued imprisonment. Because from a moral viewpoint he chooses "correctly," we must see him as a hero; his refusal to confess will, by forestalling pogroms, save countless Jewish lives. On the other hand, Bok is suffering for a negation, a return to the status quo in which Jews remain safe only until the next flare-up of anti-Semitism. If one cannot forgive God or recognize His work in one's suffering—if one's suffering shatters all faith—then in the long run there is no more reason for Bok's having to endure what he does than there was behind his being "chosen" in the first place. (See note 5 for a continuation of this discussion in regard to a later episode.)

4. Thus Bok is also forced into monologism, although some of its forms are not entirely strange to him. There is, for example, the Yiddish tendency to answer a question with a (sardonic) question or to respond with what Alan Friedman calls "Talmudic tautology," exemplified by this passage from Malamud's short story, "Take Pity":

"How did he die? . . . Say in one word."
"From what he died—he died, that's all."
"Answer, please, this question."
"Broke in him something. That's how."
"Broke what?"
"Broke what breaks." (Friedman, 289; Malamud, *Short Stories*, 7.)

I take this to be an exquisite form of monologism in that the speaker's evasions make all interchange or relationship impossible.

5. This statement about suffering seems explicit enough but it makes one wonder just what Malamud's attitude toward it is. Comparing Buber's thought to the themes of Malamud's *The Assistant*, Peter Hays said that both men believed people inevitably suffer; "to endure that suffering with as much dignity as possible is a virtue, to continue, to continue to strive to do right and to suffer for others is a mark of humanity" (Hays, 231). When the suffering is of the intensity and longevity of that of the fixer, that ideal is less than realistic. Hays says that Malamud told him that he had only a general acquaintance with Buber when he wrote *The Assistant*.

On the other hand, Kegan reports that Malamud told him that he didn't "believe in the untested spirit," that "untested, one is unrevealed." He added that it was ridiculous to claim that *The Fixer* (and *The Assistant*) were pessimistic novels (131). In his Buberian interpretation of *The Fixer*, Kegan argues that Bok initially lacks relation to the world and is therefore "spiritually destitute." By the end of the novel, Bok has become "connected." Thus for Kegan, "*The Fixer* is the story of a man who, by enduring incredible suffering in the name of an unnamed faith that there is in the world still a place for value, unconsciously denies the absurdity of existence and has awakened within him that human grace which . . . connects him to his history, and allows him as he rides into the open world to be identified" (71). This argument is plausible but not, I believe for reasons already stated, definitive.

Works Cited

Ahearn, Barry. *Zukofsky's "A." An Introduction.* Berkeley: University of California Press, 1981.
Auster, Paul. "The Decisive Moment." In *Charles Reznikoff, Man and Poet.* Ed. Milton Hindus. Orono, Maine: National Poetry Foundation, 1984.
Baker, Carlos. *Ernest Hemingway: A Life Story.* New York: Scribner's, 1969.
Baker, Carlos, ed. *Ernest Hemingway: Selected Letters, 1917–1961.* New York: Scribner's, 1981.
Bakhtin, M. M. *Problems of Dostoevsky's Poetics.* Trans. R. W. Rostel. n.p., n.d.
Bakhtin, M. M. *Rabelais and His World.* Trans. Helene Iswolsky. Cambridge: M.I.T. Press, 1968.
Bakhtin, M. M. *The Dialogic Imagination, Four Essays.* Ed. Michael Holmquist. Trans. Caryl Emerson and Michael Holmquist. Austin: University of Texas Slavic Series, 1981.
Buber, Martin. *Eclipse of God: Studies in the Relation between Religion and Philosophy.* 1932. New York: Harper Torchbooks, 1957.
Buber, Martin. *Hasidism and Modern Man.* Ed. and Trans. Maurice Friedman. New York: Harper Torchbooks, 1958.
Buber, Martin. *I And Thou.* 2d Edition. Trans. Ronald Gregor Smith. New York: Scribner's, 1958.
Buber, Martin. *The Writings of Martin Buber.* Ed. Will Herberg. New York: Meridian, 1958.

Works Cited

Buber, Martin. *Between Man and Man.* New York: Macmillan, 1965.
Buber, Martin. *The Knowledge of Man: A Philosophy of the Interhuman.* Ed. Maurice Friedman. Trans. Maurice Friedman and Ronald G. Smith. New York: Harper Torchbooks, 1966.
Buchen, Irving H. *Isaac Bashevis Singer and the Eternal Past.* New York: N.Y.U. Press, 1968.
Cahan, Abraham. *The Rise of David Levinsky.* 1917. New York: Harper Torchbooks, 1961.
Cahan, Abraham. *The Education of Abraham Cahan.* Trans. Leo Stein et al. Philadelphia: Jewish Pub. Soc. of America, 1969.
Camus, Albert. *The Stranger.* Trans. Stuart Gilbert. New York: Vintage, 1954.
Cantor, Harold. "Odets' Yinglish: The Psychology of Dialect as Dialogue." *Studies in American Jewish Literature* 2 (1982): 61–68.
Chace, William M. *The Political Identities of Ezra Pound and T. S. Eliot.* Stanford: Stanford University Press, 1973.
Chametzky, Jules. *From the Ghetto: The Fiction of Abraham Cahan.* Amherst: University of Massachusetts Press, 1977.
Dembo, L. S., and Cyrena Pondrom, eds. *The Contemporary Writer: Interviews with Sixteen Poets and Novelists.* Madison: University of Wisconsin Press, 1972.
Des Pres, Terrence. *The Survivor: An Anatomy of Life in the Death Camps.* New York: Pocket Books, 1977.
Desan, Wilfred. *The Marxism of Jean-Paul Sartre.* Garden City: Doubleday, 1965.
Diamond, Malcolm L. *Martin Buber: Jewish Existentialist.* New York: Oxford University Press, 1960.
Emery, Clark. *Ideas into Action: The Cantos of Ezra Pound.* Coral Gables: University of Miami Press, 1948.
Engel, David. "The 'Discrepancies' of the Modern: Toward a Revaluation of Cahan's *The Rise of David Levinsky.*" *Studies in American Jewish Literature* 2 (1982): 36–60.
Fiedler, Leslie. *The Jew in American Literature.* In *The Collected Essays of Leslie Fiedler.* 2 vols. New York: Stein and Day, 1970.
Freud, Sigmund. *Moses and Monotheism.* Trans. Katherine Jones. New York: Vintage, 1967.
Friedman, Alan Warren. "The Hero as Schnook." In *Bernard Malamud and the Critics.* Ed. Leslie and Judith Field. New York: New York University Press, 1970.

Friedman, Bruce Jay. *Stern.* New York: Signet, 1963.
Friedman, Bruce Jay. *His Mother's Kisses.* New York: Simon and Schuster, 1964.
Gross, Barry. "Sophie Portnoy and 'The Opposum's Death.'" *Studies in American Jewish Literature* 3 (1983): 166–78.
Grosser, Paul E., and Edwin G. Halperin. *The Causes and Effects of Anti-Semitism: The Dimensions of a Prejudice.* New York: Philosophical Library, 1978.
Harap, Louis. *In the Mainstream: The Jewish Presence in Twentieth-Century American Literature, 1950s–1980s.* Westport, Conn.: Greenwood Press, 1987.
Hatlen, Burton, ed. *George Oppen: Man and Poet.* Orono, Maine: National Poetry Foundation, 1981.
Hays, Peter L. "The Complex Pattern of Redemption." In *Bernard Malamud and the Critics.* Ed. Leslie A. and Joyce Field. New York: N.Y.U. Press, 1970. Pp. 219–34.
Hemingway, Ernest. *The Sun Also Rises.* New York: Scribner's, 1925.
Hindus, Milton. *Charles Reznikoff: A Critical Essay.* Santa Barbara: Black Sparrow, 1977.
Hindus, Milton, ed. *Charles Reznikoff: Man and Poet.* Orono, Maine: National Poetry Foundation, 1984.
Kegan, Robert. *The Sweeter Welcome, Voices for a Vision of Affirmation: Bellow, Malamud, and Martin Buber.* Needham Heights, Mass.: Humanitas Press, 1976.
Kaufmann, Walter. Prologue. *I and Thou.* By Martin Buber. Trans. Walter Kaufmann. New York: Scribner's, 1970.
Kremer, Lillian. "Dedalus in Brooklyn: Influences of *A Portrait of the Artist as a Young Man* on *My Name Is Asher Lev.*" *Studies in American Jewish Literature* 4 (1985): 84–89.
Lewis, Stuart A. "Rootlessness and Alienation in the Novels of Bruce Jay Friedman." *College Language Association Journal* 27, 3 (1975): 422–33.
Loeb, Harold. *The Way It Was.* New York: Criterion, 1959.
Liptzin, Sol. *The Jew in American Literature.* New York: Bloch, 1966.
Lyons, Bonnie. *Henry Roth: The Man and His Work.* New York: Cooper Square, 1976.
Malamud, Bernard. *The Fixer.* New York: Farrar, Strauss, 1966.
Marowitz, Sanford. "The Secular Trinity of a Lonely Millionaire: Language, Sex, and Power in *The Rise of David Levinsky.*" *Studies in American Jewish Literature* 2 (1982): 20–35.

Works Cited

Miller, David. *The New Polytheism: Rebirth of the Gods and Goddesses.* New York: Harper and Row, 1974.
Namenyi, Ernest. *The Essence of Jewish Art.* Trans. Edouard Roditi. New York: T. Yoseloff, 1960.
Oppen, George. *The Collected Poems of George Oppen.* New York: New Directions, 1974.
Oppen, Mary. *Meaning a Life: An Autobiography.* Santa Barbara: Black Sparrow, 1978.
Ozick, Cynthia. *Art and Ardor.* New York: Knopf, 1983.
Pinsker, Sanford. "The Crucifixion of Chaim Potok/The Excommunication of Asher Lev: Art and the Hasidic World." *Studies in American Jewish Literature* 4 (1985): 39–51.
Potok, Chaim. *My Name is Asher Lev.* New York: Fawcett Crest, 1972.
Pound, Ezra. *Ezra Pound Speaking: Radio Speeches of World War II.* Ed. Leonard W. Doob. Westport, Conn.: Greenwood Press, 1978.
Rachewiltz, Mary de. *Ezra Pound, Father and Teacher: Discretions.* New York: New Directions, 1983.
Rakosi, Carl. *The Collected Prose of Carl Rakosi.* Orono, Maine: National Poetry Foundation, 1983.
Reznikoff, Charles. *The Complete Poems of Charles Reznikoff.* 2 vols. Ed. Seamus Cooney. Santa Barbara: Black Sparrow, 1976 and 1977. 1: *Poems, 1918–1936.* 2: *Poems, 1937–1975.*
Rosten, Leo. *O Kaplan! My Kaplan!.* New York: Harper and Row, 1976.
Rosten, Leo. *Silky! A Detective Story.* New York: Harper and Row, 1979.
Roth, Henry. *Call It Sleep.* New York: Avon, 1964.
Roth, Philip. *Goodbye, Columbus.* New York: Meridian, 1960.
Roth, Philip. *Portnoy's Complaint.* New York: Random House, 1969.
Roth, Philip. "Writing American Fiction." In *Reading Myself and Others.* New York: Penguin, 1985. 173–92.
Sartre, Jean-Paul. *Being and Nothingness: An Essay in Phenomenological Ontology.* Trans. Hazel Barnes. New York: Philosophical Library, 1946.
Sartre, Jean-Paul. *Anti-Semite and Jew.* Trans. George I. Becker. New York: Schocken, 1948.
Sartre, Jean-Paul. "The Childhood of a Leader." *Intimacy and Other Stories.* Trans. Lloyd Alexander. New York: New Directions, 1948.

Sartre, Jean-Paul. *Nausea.* Trans. Lloyd Alexander. New York: New Directions, 1949.
Schatt, Stanley. "The Torah and the Time-Bomb: The Teaching of Jewish-American Literature Today." *College Language Association Journal* 18, 3 (1975): 434–41.
Schulz, Max F. *Radical Sophistication: Studies in Contemporary Jewish-American Novelists.* Athens: Ohio University Press, 1969.
Schulz, Max F. *Bruce Jay Friedman.* New York; Twayne, 1974.
Singer, I. B. *The Family Moskat.* Trans. A. H. Gross. New York: Farrar, 1950.
Singer, I. B. *The Manor.* Includes *The Manor* and *The Estate* in one vol. New York: Avon, 1978.
Tennenbaum, Silvia. *Rachel, the Rabbi's Wife.* New York: Morrow, 1978.
Terrell, C. F., ed. *Louis Zukofsky, Man and Poet.* Orono, Maine: National Poetry Foundation, 1979.
Torrey, E. Fuller. *The Roots of Treason: Ezra Pound and the Secret of St. Elizabeth's.* New York: Harcourt, 1984.
Uffen, Ellen Serlen. "*My Name Is Asher Lev:* Chaim Potok's 'Portrait of the Artist as a Young Hasid.' " *Studies in Jewish-American Literature* 2 (1982): 174–80.
Wallant, Edward Lewis. *The Pawnbroker.* New York: Manor, 1962.
Wallant, Edward Lewis. *The Tenants of Moonbloom.* New York: Harcourt, 1963.
Warshow, Robert. *The Immediate Experience.* New York: Atheneum, 1972.
Weiner, Deborah Heiligman. "Cynthia Ozick: Pagan Versus Jew (1966–1976)." *Studies in American Jewish Literature* 3 (1983): 179–93.
Williams, William Carlos. *The Collected Earlier Poems of William Carlos Williams.* New York: New Directions, 1951.
Williams, William Carlos. "Prologue to *Kora in Hell.*" *Selected Essays of William Carlos Williams.* New York: Random House, 1954.
Wolfenstein, Martha. "Two Types of Jewish Mothers." In *The Jews: Social Patterns of an American Group.* Ed. Marshall Sklare. Glencoe, Ill.: Free Press, 1958.
Zukofsky, Louis. *All: The Collected Short Poems, 1923–1958.* New York: Norton, 1965.

Index

Aesthetic perception. *See* Idolatry, aesthetic
Ahearn, Barry, 135
Alienation and isolation, 45, 51–53, 177*n*3.1
Anti-Semitism: in *Stern*, 7, 50; Ezra Pound's, 8, 143–51; Hemingway's, 8–9, 152–61; unmitigated evil of, 11; Sartre's views, 17–18, 21, 23–24, 29–30; 176*n*1.3; in Wallant, 50–51; in Rosten, 66–67; in Cahan, 92; in Reznikoff, 121–23, 125–26, 127; in Malamud, 162–63, 165, 166, 168, 169–70
Art, Jewish: liturgical rather than aesthetic, 107–8, 108–9, 111; events as subject of, 109–10
Assimilation, 18, 91–92, 123–24, 128–29, 130, 155. *See also* Jew, authentic and inauthentic

Baker, Carlos, 153, 153–54, 156–57
Bakhtin, M. M., 4, 9, 61, 62, 71, 81

Beiliss, Mendel, case, 10, 163, 183*n*16.1
Bellow, Saul, 162, 175–76*nIntro*.2
Bettelheim, Bruno, 167
Bloomgarden, Solomon. *See* Yehoash
Buber, Martin, 4, 4–5; concept of relation, introduced, 5, refusal of, 51–52 (*See also* Dialogue; I-Thou relation); theology of, 7; *Eclipse of God*, 15–16, 74, 110; compared with Sartre, 26, 27; concept of presence, introduced, 26–27; concept of wholeness, 26–27, 27, 29; concept of distance, 28; literary influence of, 30, 31, 175–76*nIntro*.2; *Between Man and Man*, 64–65, 107; and theories of education, 64–65, 141, 143, 182*n*14.2; views on prayer, 74–75; I-It relation in polytheism, 85, 104; God worshiped through creation, 97, 108, 133, 181*n*12.1; relation between God and Moses, 104; *The*

Index

Buber (continued)
  Knowledge of Man, 105, 107–8; and primacy of situations, 105, 108; and man's relation to things, 105–6, 106–7, 107–8; Hasidism and Modern Man, 105–6, 181n11.2,12.1.; and centrality of dialogue in Judaism, 137, 138; on duality of God, 181n11.2. See also Shekina
Buchen, Irving, 181n9.1

Cahan, Abraham: The Rise of David Levinsky, 6, 84–92, 180–81n8.1–3; absence of socialist experience in novel, 84–85, 180n8.1
Calf, golden, 4, 31–32, 103–4, 104
Camus, Albert: The Stranger, 164–66
Cantor, Harold, 71–73
Carnivalization, 4, 62–64, 66, 67, 75. See also Bakhtin
Chace, William M., 149–50
Chametzsky, Jules, 180n8.1, 181n8.3
Charmé, Stuart, 176n1.3
Communality, 29–30. See also Society
Competition as supreme value, 86–87, 90–91, 92. See also Individualism
Crucifixion, 114–15, 116, 166

Desan, Wilfred, 176n1.2
Des Pres, Terrence, 167
"Dialogic event," 26, 28, 48–50; gesture as approaching, 42–43, 98–99; between teacher and pupil, 64–65
Dialogue, 4; basis of, 27; in an authentic community, 29; spurious, 37, 86–87, 89; frustrated search for, 39–42, 45, 46, 47, 72–73; in Wallant, 47–50; Bakhtin's view of, 61; noncommunication of aesthetic vision, 114; impossibility of: in Sartre's philosophy, 27; for Holocaust survivor, 51–53
Doob, Leonard, 147–49, 151
Dostoevsky, F. M., 62
Dura Europos friezes, 109

Eliot, T. S., 110, 149; The Waste Land, 130
Emery, Clark, 146–47
Engel, David, 180n8.3
Existential Man, 5–6, 18, 19, 21, 51, 180n8.3. See also Jew, existential

Fiedler, Leslie, 152, 182–83n15.1
Formalism: introduced, 112, 138
Freud, Sigmund, 110
Friedman, Alan, 183n16.1, 2, 184n16.4
Friedman, Melvin J., 179n6.2

Gentile: monological, 7–10, 157–58, 159–60, 168–70; as evil, 162, 166. See also Anti-Semitism; Parkhill; Pound, Ezra; Hemingway, Ernest
God: hidden, 4; relation with, of observant Jew, 15, 21–22, 22–23, 30, 31–32; nonexistence of, 16–17, 22, 97, 133, 163–64, 183n16.2; Neil Klugman's prayer to, 68–69, 75; "presence" of, 74–75, 104; pantheistic, 96; worshipped through creation, 97, 108–9, 133, 181n12.1; in story of golden calf, 103–4; unitary, 104, 110;

Index

and man's relation to things, 105–6; and idea of separation into duality, 181*n11.2*
Gods and goddesses, Greek, 125–27, 128
Gold, Herbert, 70, 179*n6.2, 3*
Gold, Michael, 73
Gross, Barry, 73
Grosser, Paul E., 183*n16.1*

Halperin, Edwin G., 189*n16.1*
Harap, Louis, 11
Hasidism, 22; Buber's ideas and, 30, 105–6, 108, 181*n11.2*, 181*n12.1*; Asher Lev as Hasid, 114–16, 181*n11.2, 3*; feminine principle in, 115; Hasidic ideal in Bellow's heroes, 176*nIntro.2*
Hatlen, Burton, 136–37, 182*n13.2, 3*
Hays, Peter, 184*n16.5*
Hebrew: as uncomprehended tradition, 36; as aesthetic experience, 79–80; necessity for, for Jewish poet, 128
Hegel, G. W. F., 16, 26, 176*n1.2*
Heidegger, Martin, 15, 26, 176*n1.2*
Hemingway, Ernest: *The Sun Also Rises*, 8–9, 152–61; as Hemingstein, 156–57, 158, 161
Heraclitus, 28, 175*nIntro.1*
Holocaust, the, 9, 12, 51, 52–53, 167, 183*n16.3*
Howells, William Dean, 84
Huxley, Aldous, 108

Identity, 17; Jewish, Sartre's view of, 17–18, 21, 22–23; of Dialogical Jew, 31–32; crucial to survival in the Diaspora, 121
Idolatry, aesthetic: monologism and, 6–7, 138; story of golden calf, 103–4; religion of art, 104, 105, 108, 112–16; defined in modern world, 104–5, 108; man's relation to things, 105–6; Buber's aesthetic theory, 106; "radical aestheticizing," 107–8, 136; avoidance of, 109–11; Athena and Artemis, 124–25; Bacchus, 126–27
I-I relation, 39, 177*n3.4*. See also Solipsism
I-It relation, 4, 5, 6, 28, 29, 30–31, 85; as limit of comic novelist, 43; between man and woman, 91; in polytheism, 104; observation in, 107, 177*n2.1*. See also Buber; Monologism; Monologist; Monologue
Individualism: and loneliness, 92; and decline of family, 95, 96; as antithesis to Judaic beliefs, 113, 125; inadequacy of, 123; aloneness valued, 124; *See also* Competition as supreme value; Sartre
Isaiah, 77–78, 79, 80
I-Thou relation, 4, 5; transformation of I-It relation into, 28, 107; value in literary criticism, 30, 31; with God, 97, 108–9, 110; between God and Moses, 104. *See also* "Dialogic event"; Dialogue
It-It relation, 177*n3.4*

Jew: authentic and inauthentic, 5, 20–23, 24–25, 35–36, 154–156; alleged lack of historic past, 17–18, 21, 22; dialogical, 31–32; self-hatred of, 37–38; and non–Jewish friends, 155, 159
—conflicting identities: of Rezni-

Jew, conflicting identities *(continued)*
koff, 123–129; of Zukofsky, 130–131
—defined: 99, 136; only by anti-Semitism, 29–30, 30, 152; as ethical, 162
—existential: and Existential Man, 15, 18, 19–20; Levinsky as, 85; ostensibly observant, 94–95; Asa Heshel Bannet as, 96–97, 181*n9.1*; Bok as, 163–64, 165–67
—monological: 4, 5, 6, 32, 178*n5.2*; examples, 36, 59–61; Holocaust victim as, 51–53. *See also* Anti-Semitism
Jewishness: Sartre's images of, 5–6, 152–53; as essential to Nazerman's situation, 51–53; of Kaplan, Parkhill's inability to understand, 66; partial repudiation of, by Portnoy, 73–74; Hemingway's images of, 152, 153–54, 156–57, 159–61
—lack of heritage: of Stern, 36–37; in·Reznikoff, 122, 124
Joyce, James, 181*n11.3*
Judaism: rituals of, 36, 38, 177*n3.2*; caricature of, 36–38; Objectivist theories and, 136, 137–38; Marxism and, 136–37. *See also* God; Hasidism; Hebrew: I-Thou relation

Kaplan, Hyman (character in Rosten): 59–61, 62–67; as unfathomable anomaly, 59, 64; Columbus Day episode, 62–64
Kaufmann, Walter, 177*n3.4*
Kegan, Robert, 176*nIntro.2*, 184–85*n16.5*
Kierkegaard, Søren, 97
Klein, Carol, 179*n6.2*

Kremer, S. Lillian, 181*n11.3*

Langer, Lawrence, 9, 183*n16.3*
Language: and monologism, 3–4, 43; and dehumanization, 9; as purely social phenomenon, 28–29; as means to intimacy, 48; formal, 61; as barrier to understanding, 78–79, 138; as sacramental, 137–38; as expression of "emotional aridity," 181*n8.3*
Levinsky, David, 84; attitude toward women, 6, 87–89, 91, 180*n8.3*; values and ideals, 85–86, 86–87, 90–92, 180*n8.3*; deceptiveness, 86–87, 89
Lewis, Stuart, 177*n3.1*
Lewisohn, Ludwig, 152, 182*n15.1*
Literature and literary criticism: influence of Buber, 30, 31, 175–76*nIntro.2*; interpretive criticism, 150–51
Loeb, Harold: and Robert Cohn, 8, 9, 154–57, 159–61; *The Way It Was*, 9, 154–56
Logos: becoming mono-logos, 9, 81; Heraclitean Word, 28; and obscurity, 138
Lyons, Bonnie, 76–77, 179*n7.1*

Malamud, Bernard: *The Fixer*, 10–12, 162–71, 184–85*n16.5*; *The Assistant*, 162, 184*n16.5*; as moral allegorist, 162–63; *Short Stories*, 184*n16.4*; attitude toward suffering, 184–85*n16.5*
Marovitz, Sanford, 180*n8.3*
Marxism and socialism: Bakhtin's views and, 62; lack of influence on *The Rise of David Levinsky*, 84–85, 180*n8.1*; Pound's fascism and, 136; Judaism and, 136–37

Index

Metaphors and imagery: as perception of reality, 82–83, 112; of synagogal poetry, 109; Zukofsky on, 135
Meursault (character in *The Stranger*), 164–66
Miller, David, 110
Monologism: and aesthetic idolatry, 6–7, 138; and anti-Semitism, 7–10, 153, 157–58, 159–60, 168, 169–70; Bellow's view of, 175n*Intro.2* Monologist: loss of faith and, 3, 133–34, 136; defined, 3–4; in I-It relations, 5–6, 30–31; as sexist, 6, 55, 56–58, 87–89, 91, 180; idolator as, 7. *See also* Gentile, monological; Jew, monological
Monologue, 4; conversion into dialogue, 28; "life of," 29; quintessential example of, 45–46; solipsism in, 46–47; Bakhtin's view of, 61; disguised as dialogue, 86–87
Moonbloom, Norman, 44–45; isolation of, 45; socialization of, 47–50; irrelevance of Jewishness, 50–51
Moses, 4, 31–32, 83, 103, 104
Mother, the Jewish, 41–42, 69–74, 114–15, 178–79n6.2, 180n8.3

Namenyi, Ernest, 108–9

Objectivist poets, 110–11, 117–21, 137–38, 182n13.1–3; obscurity of, 118, 131–34, 134–36; radical aestheticism and, 136. *See also* individual poets
Odets, Clifford: *Awake and Sing!*, 70, 71
Oppen, George, 117, 118, 120, 130, 137; on Objectivism, 118,

119, 121, 150; works, 131; incomprehensibility of, 131–34, 182n13.2
Ozick, Cynthia, 104–5, 107

Paganism, 81, 95–96, 103–5, 110, 115–16; worship of Gaster, 71
Pedagogy. *See* Buber, theories of education
Pedagoguery: defined, 8, 141
Perception, 26–27, 106–7, 119; lyric valuable and, 121
Perlman, Daniel, 144
Pinsker, Sanford, 181n11.3
Polish Jews, 21, 95
Polyphony, 4, 62, 66, 79–80, 81
Polytheism, new. *See* Miller
Potok, Chaim: *My Name Is Asher Lev*, 111, 112–16, 181n11.1–3; on Buber and Hasidism, 181n12.1
Pound, Ezra, 8; fascism of, and Marxism, 136; poetics of, 136, 137–38, 142; *The Cantos*, 142; doubtful unity of, 142, 182n14.1; instinct to teach, 142–43, 143; radio speeches, 143, 147–51; antithesis in, 150
Primitivism, 115–16
Protocols of the Learned Elders of Zion, 144, 145–46, 170

Rachewiltz, Mary de, 150, 182n14.1
Rahv, Philip, 11
Rakosi, Carl, 117, 118, 118–19, 120, 137, 182n13.3
Reznikoff, Charles: on poetics of *Testimony*, 117; appeal of his poetry, 118–19; *Complete Poems*, 119–28 *passim*; finding beauty in mean objects in *Jerusalem the Golden*, 120; Babylon in *In Me-*

Index

Reznikoff (continued)
  moriam, 121; as a Jew, 121–29
Rosten, Leo: *Silky!*, 54–58; *The Education of Hyman Kaplan (O Kaplan, My Kaplan!)*, 58–67; 178n5.2
Roth, Henry: *Call It Sleep*, 76–83, 179–80n7.1, 2
Roth, Philip: *Portnoy's Complaint*, 6, 70, 73, 179n6.2, 3; *Goodbye, Columbus*, 68–70, 73–75; on Jewish-American fiction, 162–63

Samuel, Maurice, 183n16.1
Saussure, Ferdinand de, 61
Sartre, Jean-Paul, 4–5; image and knowledge of Jews, 5–6, 17–18, 24, 29–30, 153, 176n1.3; *Anti-Semite and Jew*, 5, 15–16, 23, 29–30; and Other, 5, 16, 17, 18; *Nausea*, 15, 18–19, 21, 51; *Being and Nothingness*, 16; *The Childhood of a Leader*, 23–24; *Chemins de la liberté*, 24; compared with Buber, 26, 27; principle of seriality, 176n1.2; adopted daughter (Arlette Elkaim), 176n1.3
Schulz, Max, 177n3.1
Seder, Passover, 36, 177n3.2
Shekina, 115, 181n11.2. See also Hasidism
Singer, I. B., 6, 21, 22, 25; *The Family Moskat*, 6, 93–99, 181n9.1; *The Estate*, 22
Socialism. See Marxism and Society: disintegration of, 16; concept of "seriality," 176n1.2
Solipsism, 29, 36, 39, 46–47

Spinoza, Baruch, 96, 110
Stern (character in *Stern*), 35–43; alienation of, 177n3.1; as imposter, 36, 38; obsessed desire for listener, 39–42
Suffering: meaning of, 10–11, 11, 168, 170–71, 183–84n16.3, 184–85n16.5; notion of lack of Judaic aesthetic mold for, 115

Tennenbaum, Silvia, 177n3.2, 179n6.2
Thackeray, William, 86
Tolstoy, Leo, 61
Torrey, E. Fuller, 142–43, 144, 144–45
Twitchell, Duff, 154–55, 160–61

Uffen, Ellen Serlen, 181n11.1

Wallant, Edward Lewis: *The Tenants of Moonbloom*, 3–4, 44–51; *The Pawnbroker*, 51–53, 177–78n4.1–2
Warshow, Robert, 72
Whitman, Walt, 106, 128
Williams, William Carlos, 106, 107, 118, 119–20
Wolfenstein, Martha, 178n6.2
Women: as objects, 6, 56–58, 87–89, 91, 180n8.3; idolization of, in violation of Judaism, 115. See also Mother, the Jewish

Yehoash, 130–31

Zukofsky, Louis, 117–18, 118, 120, 130–31, 134–36, 137, 150, 182n13.1